MARVEL
BLACK PANTHER

BATTLE FOR WAKANDA

SUSTAINABLE
FORESTRY
INITIATIVE

Certified Sourcing

www.sfiprogram.org
SFI-01415

MarvelHQ.com

© 2018 MARVEL. All rights reserved. Published by Marvel Press, an imprint of Disney Book Group. No part of this book may be reproduced or
transmitted in any form or by any means, electronic or mechanical, including photocopying, recording, or by any information storage or retrieval system,
without written permission from the publisher. For information address Marvel Press, 125 West End Avenue, New York, New York 10023.
Printed in the United States of America. First Paperback Edition, January 2018 10 9 8 7 6 5 4   Library of Congress Control Number: 2017906485
FAC-029261-18288 ISBN 978-1-368-02014-5

Cover illustration by Caravan Studios

STARRING

BLACK PANTHER

By **BRANDON T. SNIDER**

Illustrated by

CARAVAN STUDIOS

Los Angeles
New York

Featuring YOUR FAVORITES

BLACK PANTHER

SHURI

QUEEN RAMONDA

THE DORA MILAJE

CAPTAIN AMERICA

WAR MACHINE

CAPTAIN MARVEL

NICK FURY

KLAW

M'BAKU

THE WHITE
GORRILA CULT

VIBRANIUM

S.H.I.E.L.D
AGENTS

WAKANDA

AN IMPOSTER
BLACK PANTHER

KLAW'S SONIC
BLASTER

The Story of
BLACK PANTHER

Growing up in a royal family wasn't always easy for Prince **T'Challa.** There was great pressure to live up to the legacy of his father, T'Chaka, the respected King of Wakanda. T'Chaka was also leader of the ancient Panther Clan, a role passed down for generations. Everything changed the day an outsider named **ULYSSES KLAW**

arrived in Wakanda. He wanted to steal the country's resources for his own evil purpose. Klaw attacked T'Chaka, hitting him with one fatal blow. The loss of T'Chaka left the royal family heartbroken. As he grew older, T'Challa learned not to dwell on the the past. His calling was to become more than just a prince. He loved science. He studied hard to become a thinker and trained his mind and body to work together. T'Challa studied fighting techniques and used a unique heart-shaped herb that gave him enhanced abilities. After inventing an impenetrable suit made of a powerful element called *VIBRANIUM*, T'Challa was ready to inherit his father's title. His metamorphosis into a hero was complete. People all over the world would soon revere the powerful, the magnificent, the legendary . . .

BLACK PANTHER

you are here

In the heart of Wakanda sat a large mountain known as the Great Mound. The area held the nation's greatest resource: *VIBRANIUM*. This incredible, sound-absorbing metal had been the source of Wakanda's advanced technology for centuries. Wakandans working in the mines considered it an honor to be chosen for such a role. Today, however, many of them did not feel very honored.

"Look out!" a miner shouted.

TICK, TICK, TICK... BOOM!

An explosion rocked the Great Mound as the White Gorilla Cultists stormed the area. They were led by a fearsome warlord known as **M'Baku,** who directed his mercenaries to destroy everything. Their savagery was known throughout Wakanda. However, their exact motives remained unclear. They hadn't stolen anything, nor had they before. Their only mission, it seemed, was to terrify.

"Run for your lives!" another miner yelled.

Terrified workers scattered in all directions as cultists ravaged the area. Pandemonium overtook the Mound as miners desperately defended themselves against the brutal attack.

A cultist raised his spear high into the air above an innocent miner, but before he could land a blow, a silent black streak darted across the Great Mound at lightning speed.

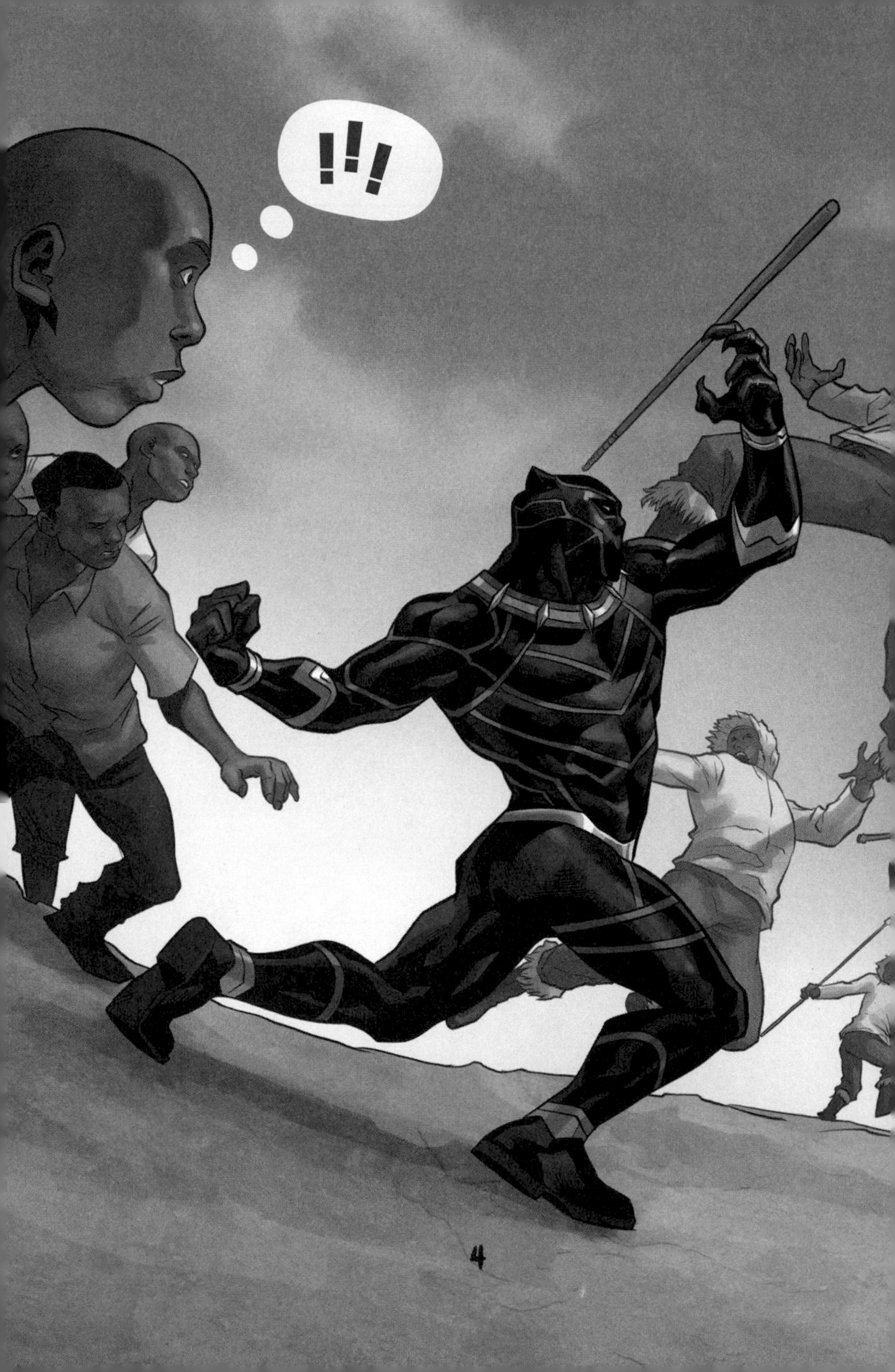
!!!

It was the **BLACK PANTHER**, and he was angry. He pounced on the cultist, ripping the spear from his hand and tossing him through the air!

The fallen cultist scoffed. **"You have no idea what's coming."**

The ominous warning struck fear in Black Panther's heart. Avengers business had kept him busy. He'd been spending more time outside of Wakanda than he was used to, and it left him feeling as if he didn't know what was going on inside his own country.

"What do you want?" Black Panther growled.

"You'll see," the cultist sneered.

"Where is M'Baku?" Black Panther asked. Before he could answer, a new commotion swept through the Mound.

"Clear out!" a cultist roared. The cultists were retreating. They'd released a smoke bomb that coated the area in a thick cloud of fog to mask their exit.

As the smoke cleared, Black Panther was left with even more questions.

"Is everyone all right?" Black Panther asked the miners.

"No!" a voice shouted. **"We are not all right!"** An angry miner named Ato barreled to the front of the throng.

"Speak freely, Ato, so that you may be heard," Black Panther said.

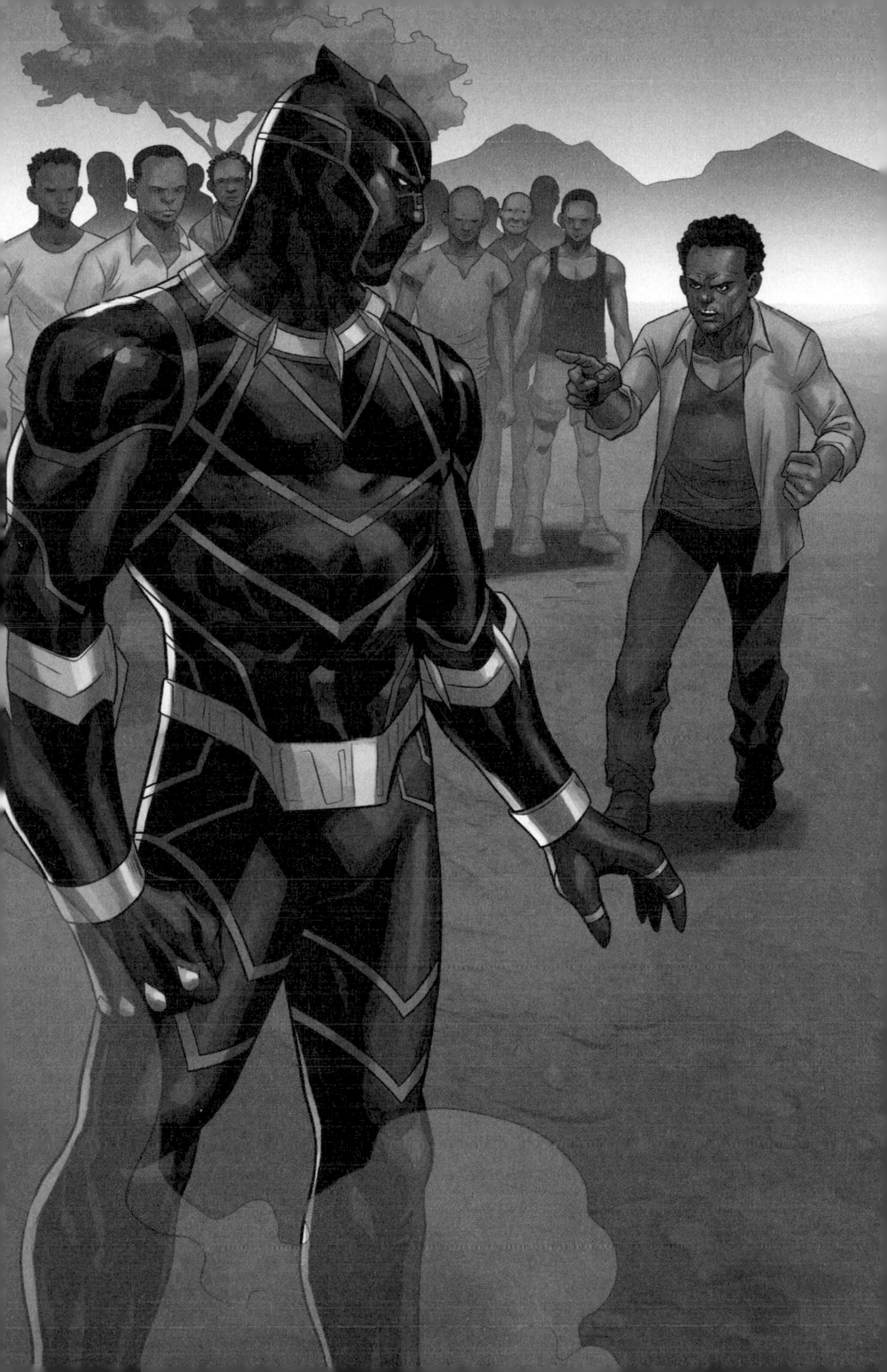

Ato's body tensed as he described the situation.

"These White Gorilla Cultists have attacked the Great Mound three times in the past month. And for what?!" Ato shouted.

He paced back and forth with a nervous energy. **"They do not steal our Vibranium. Why then do they attack? When will this violence stop?!"** Ato looked at his fellow miners for approval. He hoped they, too, would speak up, but the crowd hung their heads low and remained silent.

Ato turned his attention back to Black Panther. **"Where have you been, dear king? Do you not know what is happening in your own kingdom?"**

Black Panther prided himself on being a kind and approachable leader. He wasn't used to being confronted with such anger from one of his own people. Ato's frustration was unmistakable. Black Panther wondered if his response would be enough. He considered his words carefully before speaking. **"I'm aware of these previous assaults. I understand the terrible toll they've taken. I'm currently investigating the situation,"** he explained.

"Ha!" Ato cackled. He turned, pointing to the other frustrated miners. **"And you think this brings us comfort? We need a leader. Meanwhile, our king is too busy being a Super Hero."**

Ouch!

Ato's words stung. Black Panther cared deeply for the Wakandan people and had always done what he felt was in their best interest. Being an Avenger and defending the Earth was part of that mission. Now he wasn't so sure it was the best course of action.

"Your father was devoted to his country. He died protecting it," Ato said.

Black Panther's anger began to rise. **"I love this country and will do anything to protect its people."**

"Prove it," Ato said.

"Enough!" Black Panther turned and addressed the crowd with authority. **"It's true that I have a life outside our nation. I'm proud to walk among Earth's Mightiest Heroes, but hear me when I say they do not own me. I am not at their beck and call."**

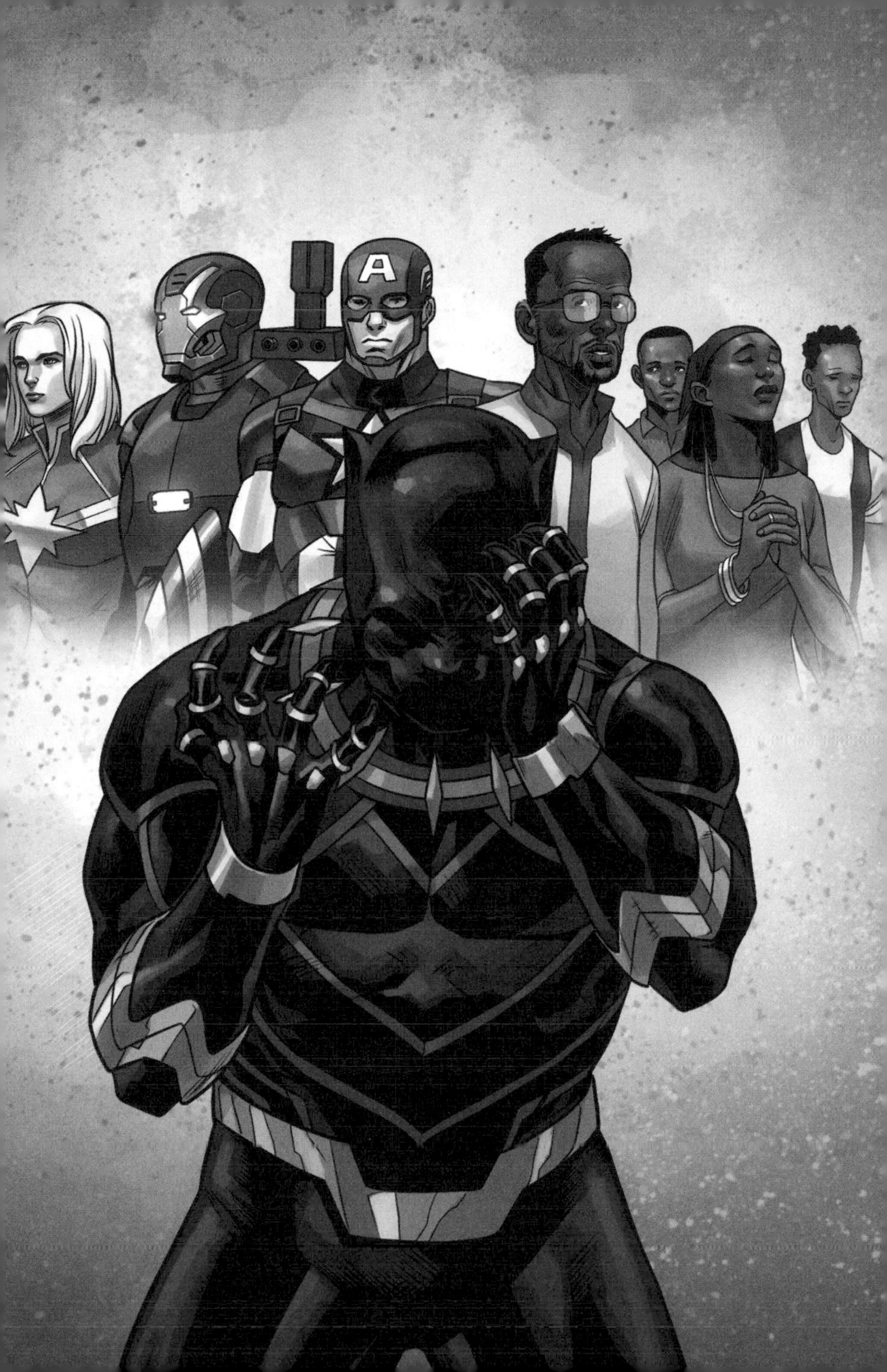

FWOOOOM!!! A mechanical roar sounded in the distant sky, moving closer by the second. It was the Quinjet, chosen mode of transportation for **the Avengers**. The craft landed on the edge of the Great Mound as the assembled miners stared with curiosity.

"Do you see? Do you see? Our king's masters are here to collect him," Ato said, turning to the other miners. "These people and their ugly spacecrafts. A Wakandan could create something ten times better."

The ship's door opened as Captain Marvel, Captain America, and *WAR MACHINE* stepped out.

"LOOKS LIKE YOU'VE GOT A REAL PARTY GOING ON HERE," War Machine joked. Black Panther's eyes narrowed.

"I'm dealing with a situation that requires my full attention. What brings you to Wakanda?" he asked.

"We need to speak with you," Captain America said. **"We wouldn't have come all this way if it wasn't important."**

Ato released a hearty chuckle. **"Then it is confirmed!"** he said, turning to the crowd once again. **"Do you not see? He is owned by these Avengers. Our king serves another master."**

Captain America turned to Black Panther and gently grabbed his arm. **"Is there a place we can speak privately?"** he asked.

"We'll go to the capital,"
Black Panther said, pulling away
from his grip. "To the royal palace."

"Yes, go to your shimmering palace,
away from the people," Ato said.

Ato's rudeness agitated Captain Marvel.
"Watch it, buddy!" she shouted. "Black Panther is
still your king!"

Ato sneered and picked up his broken tools as the crowd dispersed. Black Panther was impressed with his people's continued resilience in the face of danger. ***I will get to the bottom of this***, he thought. The Avengers headed toward the Quinjet for the short journey to the capital of Wakanda.

War Machine noticed Black Panther's frustration and tried to lighten the mood. **"TOUGH CROWD, MAN,"** he said with a smile.

"I can't believe you let that guy talk to you like that," Captain Marvel said.

"I didn't let him *do* anything. I merely listened," Black Panther said. **"Respect isn't demanded, Captain. It's earned."**

"You got that right!" Captain Marvel replied.

Black Panther pulled Captain America aside to speak privately as the others boarded the ship.

"The people are tense. My duties as an Avenger have kept me away from my duties as the King of Wakanda. A mysterious enemy has chosen to take advantage of this. It's a matter I look forward to handling on my own."

Captain America nodded.

At the royal palace, the Avengers made themselves comfortable in Black Panther's personal quarters. The modern space was filled with ancient relics from Wakanda's past. A portrait of his father when he was the reigning Black Panther hung in the middle of the room. Black Panther treasured it above all else. War Machine removed his helmet and strolled through the room, looking at each piece of history.

"NICE PLACE YOU'VE GOT HERE," he said. *"NEED A ROOMMATE?"*

"You're always welcome to *visit*," Black Panther said, grinning under his mask. **"It's not often that I receive guests."**

Captain Marvel had grown tired of pleasantries. **"Let's get down to business, Panther,"** she said. **"Last night, a** guy dressed like you robbed a top secret S.H.I.E.L.D. black site. We know you didn't do it, but Nick Fury still wants us to bring you in for questioning."

"I don't understand," Black Panther said. "I've been in Wakanda for over a week now since our last mission. Fury knows this. S.H.I.E.L.D. should be able to solve this mystery easily and without my involvement."

"THERE'S A GUY OUT THERE COMMIT-TING CRIMES DRESSED EXACTLY LIKE YOU," War Machine offered. "AREN'T YOU AT LEAST WORRIED?"

Black Panther was annoyed. "Villains are invading my country. The people of Wakanda feel threatened, and I haven't been here to protect them. That worries me more than anything else right now."

Captain America took a deep breath, and he explained the situation as he saw it. "I understand your predicament, T'Challa. I truly do. But believe me when I tell you—S.H.I.E.L.D. isn't asking. This is not a request."

"Then it's an order?" Black Panther replied. "What if I choose not to come with you?"

"We answer to S.H.I.E.L.D. That's the way it is. You signed up for stuff like this when you joined the Avengers!" Captain Marvel said, her temper flaring. "There are no free rides. Even for kings."

22

Black Panther wanted to honor his commitment to the Avengers, but he'd also made a commitment to defend his people. There was a serious choice before him, and he wasn't sure what to do.

Before he could answer, **Ramonda,** the Queen Mother, walked into the room. She smiled. **"No one told me we had guests. I would've had the chef prepare a snack for everyone."**

Noting that they were in the presence of royalty, Captain America, War Machine, and Captain Marvel bowed.

But Ramonda wouldn't have such a thing. **"Rise. Please. This tradition has always made me uncomfortable,"** she explained. Ramonda embraced the Avengers, giving them each a warm and sturdy hug. **"What brings you to Wakanda? Taking my son away on a new adventure?"**

"Someone has taken my identity and used it to commit a crime. My colleagues are here to bring me in for questioning," Black Panther said. The room fell silent.

"May I have a moment alone with my stepson, please?" Ramonda asked.

"Of course," said Captain America.

The Avengers respectfully stepped out of the room.

"It's good to have you home," Ramonda said.

"It's good to be home," said Black Panther. "I'm pulled in many directions these days, as you well know."

"T'Challa, do me a favor and remove your mask," Ramonda said. "I want to see your face when I'm speaking to you."

The Black Panther's uniform was made of a bulletproof Vibranium weave that protected him from harm. It did not, however, prevent him from facing reality. He removed his mask and smiled at his stepmother.

Ramonda put her hand to T'Challa's cheek and grinned. "My proud son. The king," she said. "Heavy is the head that wears the crown."

"How many times must I hear that tired old phrase?" T'Challa asked. He turned to look at a Wakandan artifact on display. "There's

unrest at the Great Mound," he said. "**The White Gorilla Cultists have reared their ugly heads yet again.**"

"**Do you have any leads?**" Ramonda asked.

"**No,**" T'Challa answered. "**It's infuriating.**"

"Utilize all your resources. There are

answers to your questions," Ramonda said. "In the meantime, know that Wakanda is forever grateful for your protection."

T'Challa shook his head. "**You don't understand. The people think I'm abandoning them**," he said. "**They think my duties as an Avenger come before their needs. I wonder if they're right.**"

"You've helped the Avengers fight madmen that would destroy the entire planet, Wakanda included," said Ramonda. "Surely the people understand that."

"**It's not enough for them**," said T'Challa. "**The people speak only of my failures.**"

"And what of your achievements?" Ramonda said. "Remember the good that you're doing."

Stepmother and stepson gazed out across the vastness of their kingdom and were met with a feeling of calmness as they recalled fond times from the past.

"Your father would have been so proud of you. This is not an easy job. Your father knew that more than anyone," said Ramonda. She rested her head on T'Challa's shoulder.

T'Challa knew what he had to do. **"I'll accompany the Avengers to the S.H.I.E.LD. Helicarrier and return as quickly as possible,"** he said. There was a renewed firmness in his voice. **"Then I will get to the bottom of these attacks and stop them once and for all. I owe Wakanda everything I have,"** he said. **"I won't let my people down."**

"Is everything OKAY?"

Shuri, T'Challa's sister, rushed into the room. "I was combat training when the cultists attacked. I came as soon as I heard. Also—is that a Quinjet parked outside?"

Despite her role as princess of Wakanda, Shuri was unconcerned with the flourishes of her royal stature. She preferred the heat of battle and had been training for it since she was a little girl.

"Shuri, my dear, your brother's friends are here," Ramonda said. "How was your training session?"

"Learned a few new moves. You can tell the Avengers I'm ready if ever they need me, brother." Shuri grinned.

Shuri's playful suggestion gave T'Challa an idea. When she wasn't busy with her studies, Shuri developed her skills as a fighter by watching the **Dora Milaje,** Wakanda's royal guard. "Shuri, listen closely. I must leave Wakanda again. I need you to lead in my stead," he said.

Shuri's eyes widened at the prospect.

"You'll have the Dora Milaje at your disposal. Should the White Gorilla Cult attack again, I need you to rally your forces. Can you do that for me?" T'Challa asked.

"T'Challa, I don't . . ." Shuri stuttered. "You're the chosen one. You're the Black Panther, not me. I'm just a girl who dreams of being a hero."

"You are yourself," T'Challa said. "That's all I need you need to be."

Shuri looked at Ramonda for approval. "Is that all right, Mother?" she asked.

"Always," Ramonda said. "You both fill my heart with pride."

T'Challa hugged his sister tight. "Stay vigilant. Be prepared. Wakanda is counting on you," he said. "Oh, and make sure you leave your communicator on in case I need to reach you."

Shuri couldn't believe her luck. She worked hard to suppress an excited giggle. "I won't let you down," she said.

There was a light TAP! TAP! TAP! on the door. Captain

Marvel poked her head into the room to check in. "What's the verdict?" she asked T'Challa. "Are you ready to do this?"

"To be clear—you've asked me to join you to prove myself innocent of a crime I plainly did not commit," T'Challa said. "I was under the impression that membership in the Avengers afforded me a level of respect. Now my loyalties are questioned. Tell me, Captain America, what would you do?"

Captain America chose his words carefully. "I get it, T'Challa. I honestly do. S.H.I.E.L.D. can be frustrating. Their actions don't always sit well with me. I respect you and your royal stature. Your unwavering heroism is the reason I'm proud to call you my teammate. We need that heroism to help find this imposter

and stop him. Once this is all said and done, the Avengers will help you take down the cultists for good. You have my word."

T'Challa admired Captain America's leadership during their time on the battlefield, but they were in Wakanda now. The king made sure he remembered that. **"I follow no one blindly, Captain. And you didn't answer my question."**

"We've got your back," Captain Marvel said. **"Don't worry."**

34

T'Challa sighed. There was only one solution to this problem. **"I shall join the Avengers in clearing my name and return to Wakanda at once,"** he said, putting his mask on again.

Let's make this quick.

CHAPTER 3

The Avengers boarded the Quinjet and prepared to leave Wakanda. But before it took off, Shuri ran to her brother's side.

"How long will you be gone?" she asked.

"As long as it takes to clear my name," Black Panther answered. Shuri suddenly seemed anxious. The gravity of taking on her brother's responsibilities had finally hit her. **"You'll do fine, Shuri. Trust me,"** he reassured her.

Captain Marvel nodded from the cockpit of

the Quinjet, signaling that it was time to go. Black Panther joined his fellow Avengers, waving at Shuri from the window.

"Be safe, brother," Shuri whispered to the sky.

Aboard the Quinjet, Black Panther, Captain Marvel, and War Machine gathered around a holographic video display as Captain America briefed the team. **"This footage was taken at a S.H.I.E.L.D. installation somewhere in the United States. The location is highly classified,"** he explained. **"Even I don't know."**

imposter

"S.H.I.E.L.D. and their secrets," Black Panther said.

The group watched as an individual dressed exactly like Black Panther stealthily made his way around the perimeter of the ordinary-looking site.

He swiftly took out two **S.H.I.E.L.D.** agents with a barrage of intense, focused strikes.

imposter!

"This guy is good," Captain Marvel said.

The group watched as the imposter entered the facility. He was looking for something. Soon he discovered a private laboratory, filled with numerous mechanical devices. The imposter scanned the area and soon found his prize:

a thin metal bracelet. Four more **S.H.I.E.L.D.** agents entered the room. The Avengers watched as the imposter mimicked Black Panther's fighting style to the letter. After defeating the agents, the imposter snatched the metal bracelet.

"Zoom in on that bracelet," Black Panther said. **"What does it do?"**

"That is top secret," Captain America answered. **"S.H.I.E.L.D. won't tell us. We can assume it's very dangerous."**

Before the imposter slipped away into the night, he stopped and stared directly into the closed-circuit camera.

"He knows he's being watched," Black Panther said.

"AND HE DOESN'T SEEM TO MIND," War Machine added.

Captain America ended the surveillance video.

"Do you believe that I've committed this crime?" asked Black Panther.

"Of course not," Captain America said.

Black Panther became agitated. "Your justification is lacking, Captain. You know I've been in my homeland. It's easily verifiable. S.H.I.E.L.D. has an entire Helicarrier filled with technology. Tell them to use it," he exclaimed. "I'm done here. Take me back to Wakanda at once."

"There's one more thing you need to know," Captain America explained. "S.H.I.E.L.D. found your DNA at the scene of the crime."

"How is that even possible?" Captain Marvel asked.

Black Panther thought of himself as a team player, but he'd begun to wonder if joining the Avengers was more trouble than it was worth. He trusted his colleagues but he didn't trust **S.H.I.E.L.D.** Despite his rising anger, Black Panther did his best to remain calm. **"Someone is framing me. That much is clear. What does Nick Fury think? Surely he has theories regarding this situation."**

"I've worked with Nick Fury for many years. He won't discuss specifics. This is a sensitive situation and his reasons are his own. Having said that, I was able to put together some clues based on what I know of all current and active S.H.I.E.L.D. investigations," Captain America said.

"COME ON. SPILL IT, CAP," War Machine

said. *"WHAT ARE WE UP AGAINST HERE?"*

Captain America activated a holographic image of Baron Zemo. **"Zemo may have been involved in some way. S.H.I.E.L.D. has been keeping an eye on him for a while now. There's a rumor he's been collecting weapons of all sorts,"** he explained.

"NOTHING NEW THERE," War Machine said.

"Unfortunately, it's all we've got for the moment," Captain America said. **"Once we arrive at the Helicarrier, I hope we'll receive some new and better information."**

Black Panther's confusion increased. **"I have no quarrel with Zemo. Why then would he seek to set me up?"**

"Because he's a jerk," Captain Marvel offered. *"HE PROBABLY DIDN'T GET ENOUGH HUGS*

43

WHEN HE WAS A KID," War Machine said.

Black Panther was tired of jokes.

"I'll meet with Fury to prove my inno- cence," Black Panther said. **"Then we'll find this imposter and end this."**

"That's the spirit," Captain America said. **"You'll be home in no time."**

BEEP! BEEP! BEEP!

The Quinjet received an incoming transmis- sion from **Nick Fury** himself.

"**Speak of the devil,**" Captain Marvel said.

Fury's eyes lit up. "**Black Panther, it's good to see you. Wouldn't you know it, you're robbing one of my facilities right this very moment. It's a former A.I.M. hideout. I had S.H.I.E.L.D. shut it down a while back. There's a lot of nasty stuff in this place. Being as busy as I am, I haven't had a chance to clean it out yet. Would you guys mind making a pit stop before coming to say hello? Oh, and bring that imposter back with you, too. I've got a few questions for him.**"

Black Panther's eyes narrowed.

"**My pleasure.**"

not Black Panther

CHAPTER 4

The imposter Black Panther was in the middle of a fight against a handful of **S.H.I.E.L.D.** agents.

"Freeze!" an agent shouted. He drew his weapon and the imposter kicked it out of his hand. Two more agents tried to subdue the imposter. He grabbed them by the arms and tossed them into the air like sandbags. Thankfully the Avengers arrived to provide a helping hand.

"GOTCHA!" War Machine exclaimed. He

swooped in to save the agents then deposited them safely on the ground below.

The Black Panther imposter spotted the Avengers closing in on him. Suddenly he whipped around, digging his claws into the steel door behind him. He ripped it off, fleeing deeper inside the building.

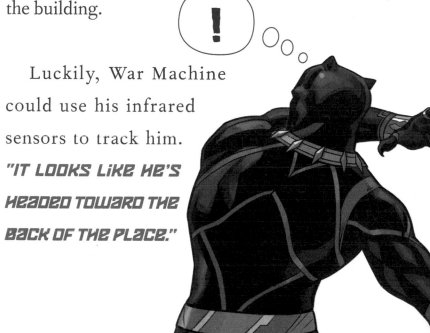

Luckily, War Machine could use his infrared sensors to track him. **"IT LOOKS LIKE HE'S HEADED TOWARD THE BACK OF THE PLACE."**

"Clear out! This might get messy."

Captain Marvel shouted.

She cracked her knuckles and barreled through the building like a battering ram, slamming through walls as if they were made of paper.

The Avengers followed closely behind as she punched her way through layer after layer of thick metal till she reached their destination; a hidden lab deep within the facility. It contained bizarre alien inventions and half-assembled devices.

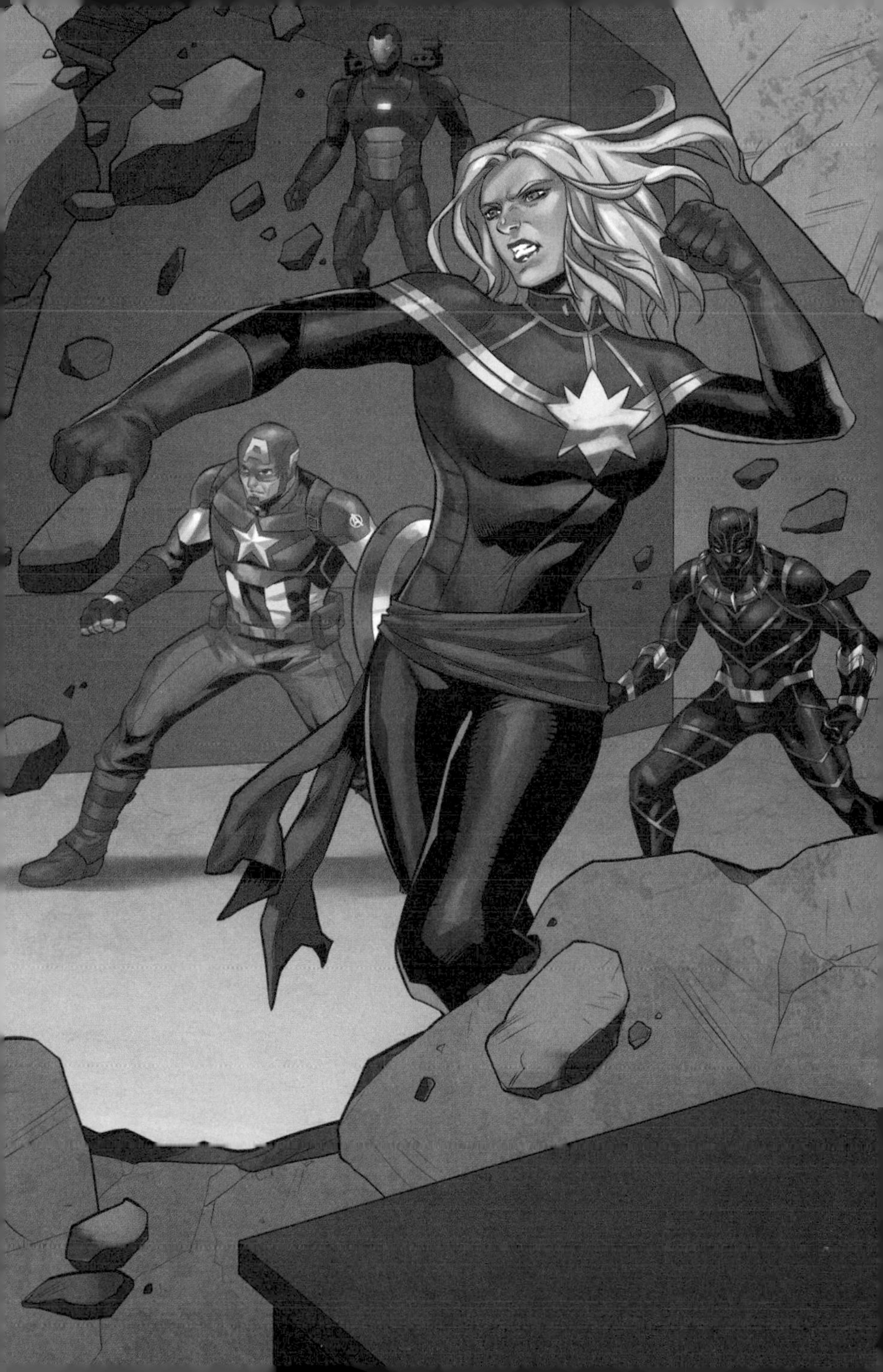

Wires, circuit boards, and other assorted electronics were scattered across the room. When the heroes entered, they saw the imposter Black Panther frantically searching through a group of toppled metal boxes. Finally, he found the device he was looking for, clutching it in his hand. He whipped around at the sound of a booming voice coming from behind him.

"Sorry to rain on your parade, freak," Captain Marvel said, confidently placing her hands on her hips. **"But unfortunately we're going to have to destroy you now. Personally, I think one Black Panther is enough. There's only so much silent brooding I can take."**

The imposter narrowed his eyes. He was cornered. In front of him were three Avengers who were ready to pounce. Behind him was a giant digital screen covered in complicated schematics. There was nowhere left to run.

War Machine looked around, confused. "HEY GUYS, UM, WHERE'S THE REAL--?"

Suddenly a pair of clawed hands ripped through the digital screen behind the imposter. Black Panther pounced and sent the imposter flying with one powerful punch!

WHAM!

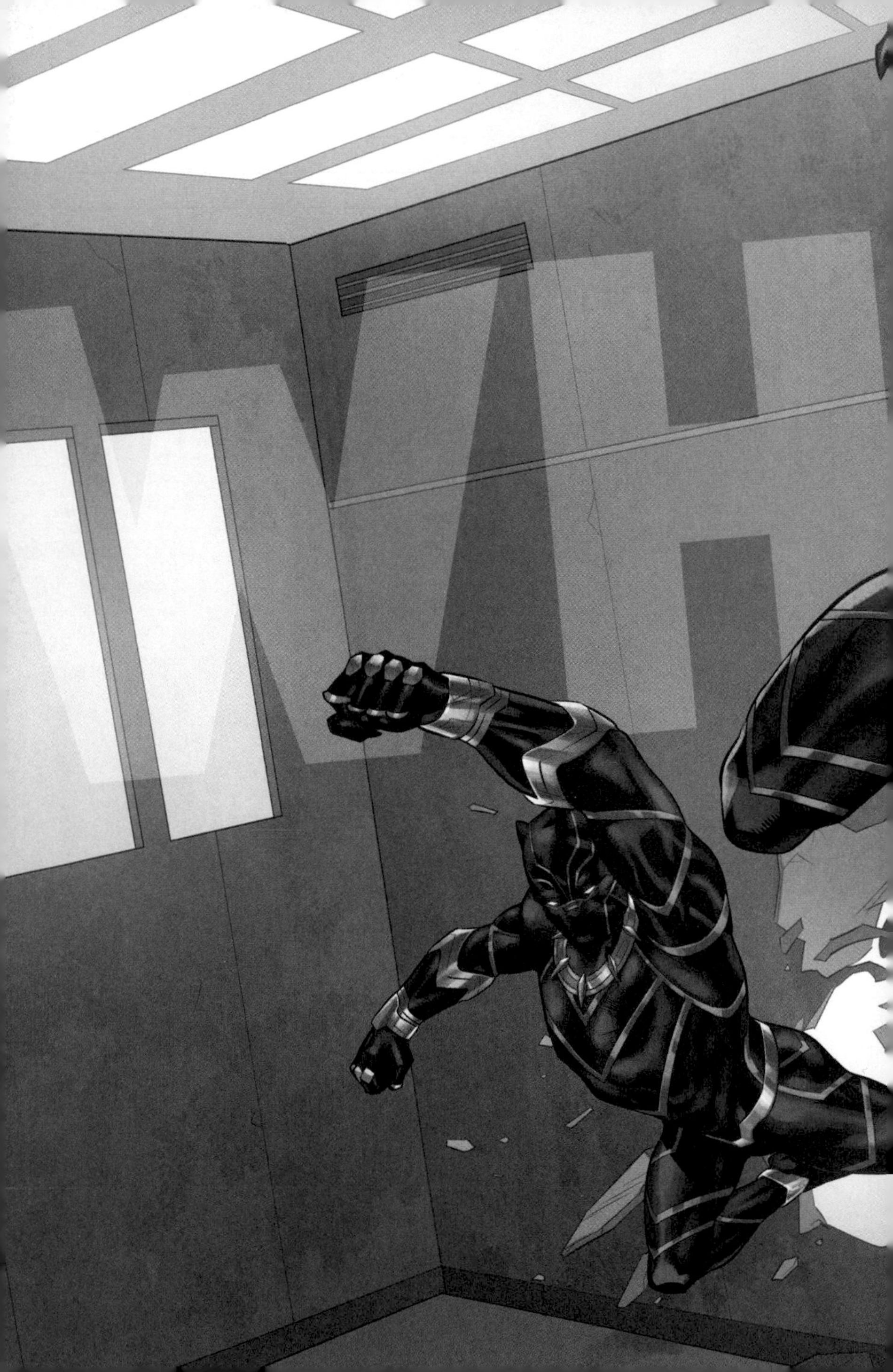
WH

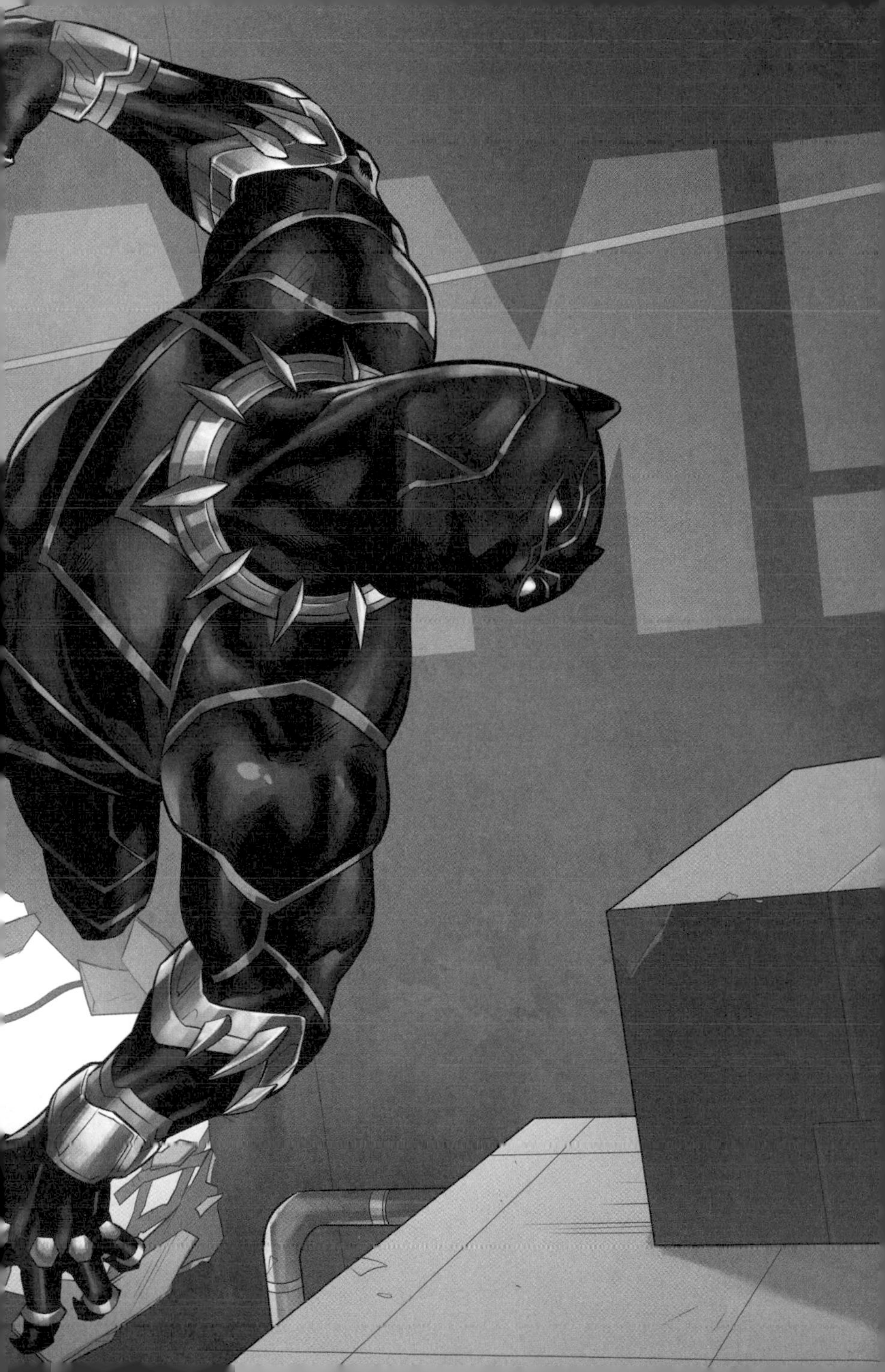

"You put up quite a fight," Black Panther said as the villain lay unconscious. **"Time to see who you really are."** He pulled off the imposter's mask to reveal a face identical to his own.

"HE'S STILL ALIVE, RIGHT?" War Machine asked.

Captain America eyed the lifeless body with curiosity. **"He never was."**

"WHAT?! BUT HOW?" War Machine said. *"T'CHALLA, IF YOU HAVE A SECRET EVIL TWIN TELL US NOW!"*

"It's a S.H.I.E.L.D. Life Model Decoy," Captain

is this dude for real?

America said, stunned by the sudden realization.

"What's a Life Model Decoy?" Black Panther said.

"It's a highly sophisticated robot. It knows speech patterns and body language. It can also mimic thoughts," Captain America explained. **"It's even got your fingerprints and DNA, which explains why they found some at the scene of the first break-in."**

"Why is there a Black Panther version?" Captain Marvel asked.

"It looks like S.H.I.E.L.D. has some explaining to do. Another metal bracelet? I wonder what the connection might be," Cap said.

Black Panther remained silent. He boiled with frustration over the mess he'd found himself in. **"I would have words with Nick Fury. Take me to the Helicarrier. Now."**

CHAPTER

5

The **S.H.I.E.L.D.** Helicarrier moved through the clouds keeping a watchful eye on the world below. Stomping through the long corridors, it was clear to Black Panther that **S.H.I.E.L.D.** could never be trusted. They played by their own rules.

"Explain this!" Black Panther shouted as he tossed the limp body of the imposter at Nick Fury's feet.

"Thanks for returning my property," Fury said. **"I was wondering where he ran off to."**

Fury nodded to two **S.H.I.E.L.D.** agents. They picked the body up and placed it on a steel table.

"You knew what this was all along," Captain America said.

"I had my suspicions, but in this business, one never knows what to expect," Fury said.

"This thing tried to kill us!" Captain Marvel said.

"Someone else was controlling it, not **S.H.I.E.L.D.** Life Model Decoys aren't easy to program. Whoever did this must be one smart cookie," said Fury. "And, Captain Marvel, I'd mind your tone if I were you. You destroyed a lot of **S.H.I.E.L.D.** property today."

"SHE WAS TRYING TO CATCH THIS GUY," War Machine said. *"THE GUY YOU SENT US TO CATCH."*

"At ease, everyone. We're all on the same team here," Fury said.

"Enough!" Black Panther shouted. **"You lie and manipulate to get what you want, Fury, but you will not deceive the King of Wakanda. Speak plainly and tell me the truth."**

"The truth is complicated," Fury said. "We're more alike than you think, Panther. Think of S.H.I.E.L.D. as my kingdom. I would do anything to protect it. You catch my drift?"

A **S.H.I.E.L.D.** agent entered the bridge.

"Excuse me for a moment, Avengers," Fury said as he turned. **"How are things on the cellblock, agent? Is Klaw adjusting to his new surroundings?"**

KLAW. The name made Black Panther's skin crawl. When Black Panther was just a boy, he watched Ulysses Klaw murder his father after Klaw attempted to steal Wakanda's supply of Vibranium. The terrible sight scarred him deeply. Even with the support of his step-mother and sister, he never fully recovered from his father's passing. In an impulsive act, young T'Challa stole one of Klaw's own sound blasters and used it against him. The device destroyed

name: KLAW, ULYSSES
current alias: KLAW
gender: Male
height: 5' 11"
weight: 175 lbs
status: INCARCERATED –
THE RAFT//TRANSFER//
S.H.I.E.L.D. HQ
charge(s):
• ARMED ROBBERY
• BREAKING AND
ENTERING

Klaw's right hand, which he replaced with a powerful sonic weapon. He then embarked on a vengeful quest to destroy T'Challa. Though they hadn't faced each other in quite some time, Klaw's presence made Black Panther unsettled.

"What's Klaw doing here?" the Panther asked.

"He's a recent transfer from the Raft," Fury explained. **"Don't worry. He's not going anywhere."**

"Back to the matter at hand," Captain America

said. "**Give it to me straight, Nick. Helmut Zemo is behind this, isn't he?**"

Fury paced back and forth. "**I'm unable to confirm or deny. You know that, Cap. Look, I'm very grateful that you were able to find my missing equipment. Thank you all for coming. We'll take it from here.**"

Black Panther stepped into Fury's path. "**Why did you create a duplicate of me?**"

"**You're a very powerful man, T'Challa,**" Fury answered.

"**This entire room is filled with powerful men and women. You evade the question,**" Black Panther explained.

Fury stared Black Panther down. "**It was a precaution. Don't worry. He won't get loose again,**" he said. "**Trust me.**"

"Trust is the last thing I have in this organization," Black Panther scoffed.

Captain America placed the stolen devices on the table beside the Life Model Decoy. "This is what it took," he said. "Two metal bracelets. Not sure what they do."

"WHAT NOW?" War Machine asked.

Fury pondered the question. "Now we find out who's been controlling this guy," he said. As Fury leaned in to get a closer look, the Life Model Decoy grabbed him by the neck and tossed him through the air. The decoy launched itself off the table, landing squarely on its feet. It snatched the two bracelets, vaulted itself over a balcony, and took off running down a corridor.

Black Panther seethed. He took off after it, leaping off the walls to push himself forward.

Faster and faster, the two Black Panthers raced down the empty corridor at top speed. They chased each other around the winding metal hallways until they reached a dead end. The decoy lunged, swinging its sharp claws through the air with wild abandon. Black Panther dodged each swipe with ease.

The decoy swept its foot across the floor.
Black Panther leaped into the air to avoid it.
They grappled, straining with force as each one
attempted to gain the upper hand. The Avengers
soon arrived on the scene to find two Black
Panthers locked in combat before them.

"**WHICH ONE OF THESE GUYS IS OUR
FRIEND?**" War Machine asked.

Captain America struggled to answer.
"**I don't know.**"

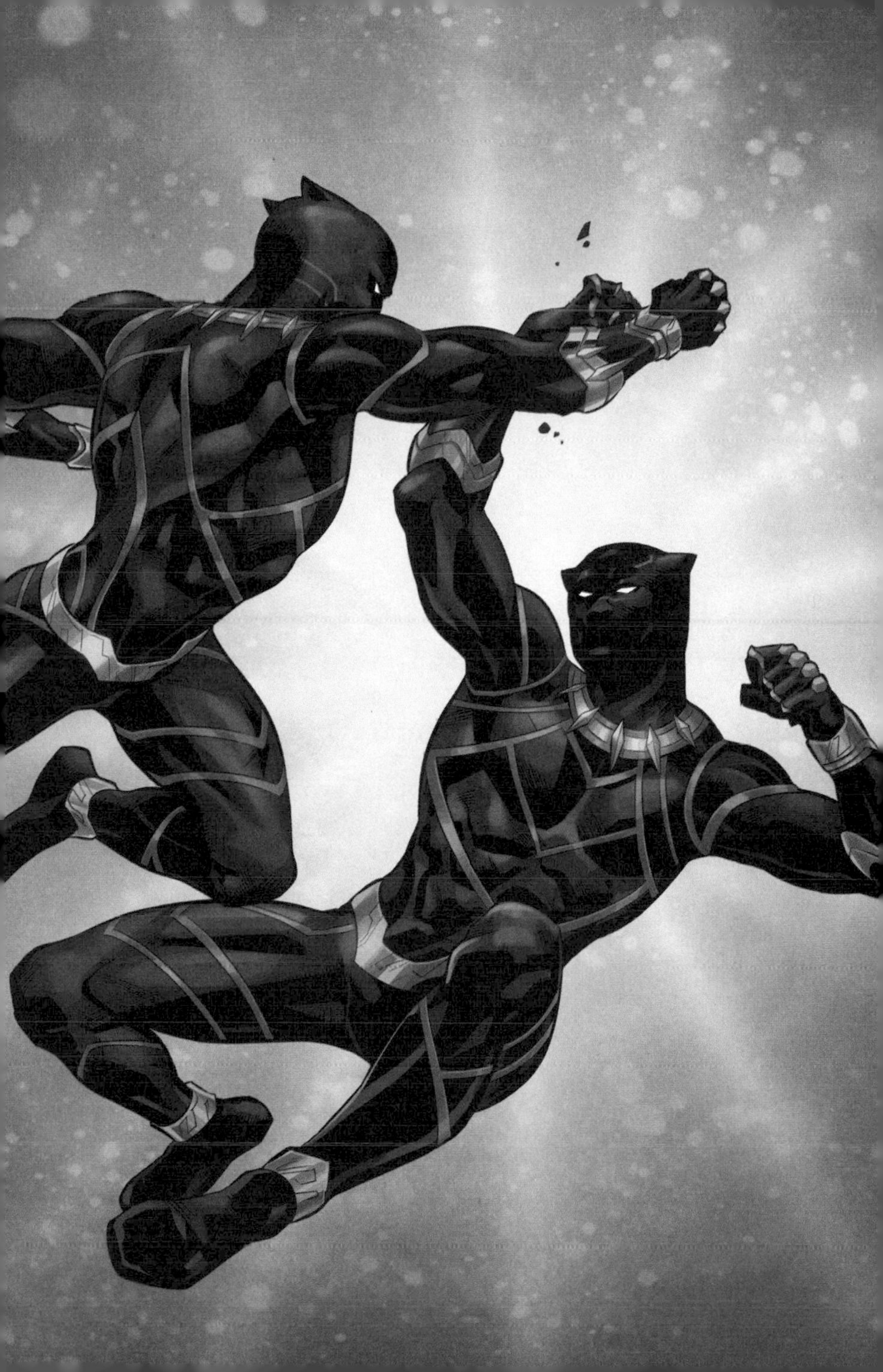

CHAPTER

6

Black Panther was in the fight of his life against the evil Life Model Decoy. The Avengers had no idea which one was which. One Black Panther head-butted the other before giving him a brutal punch to the gut.

"Ouch," Captain Marvel whispered. **"What do we do? Watch and wait?"**

"I KNOW HOW TO TELL THEM APART," War Machine said. He activated his launcher and took aim. He fired a rocket, blasting through a wall

and leaving behind a gaping hole. The decoy
saw its chance at escape and took it.

"*now we know,*" War Machine said.

"**Where exactly does he think he's going?**" Captain
Marvel asked. "**We're on a giant sky ship. It's not like
he has a lot of options.**"

"*beats me,*" War Machine said. "*you okay,
panther?*"

Black Panther dusted his shoulders off. "**I'm
fine,**" he said, jumping through the hole.

The decoy encountered a battalion of armed **S.H.I.E.L.D.** agents but remained unfazed. It looked up and swung himself onto a balcony ledge. The agents fired into the air after him. But the decoy ran down the catwalk. He knew where it was going. Then it leaped off and landed on another catwalk, lower down. The Avengers followed close behind, spotting it down below. **"There he is!"** shouted

Captain Marvel. The decoy ran to a big red door, threw it open, and went inside.

"OH NO," War Machine said. *"THAT'S NOT GOOD."*

"What's behind that door?" Black Panther asked.

"THAT LEADS TO THE CELLBLOCK."

The Black Panther decoy scoped out each cell. Once it found the right one, the decoy smashed through the control panel, which opened the cell door. Its criminal occupant stepped out in a dramatic fashion.

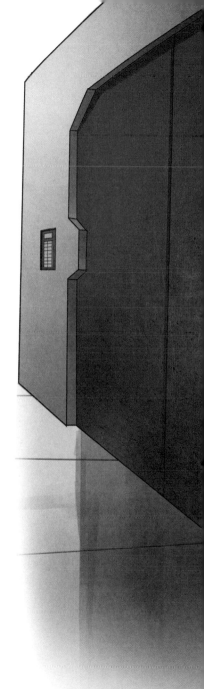

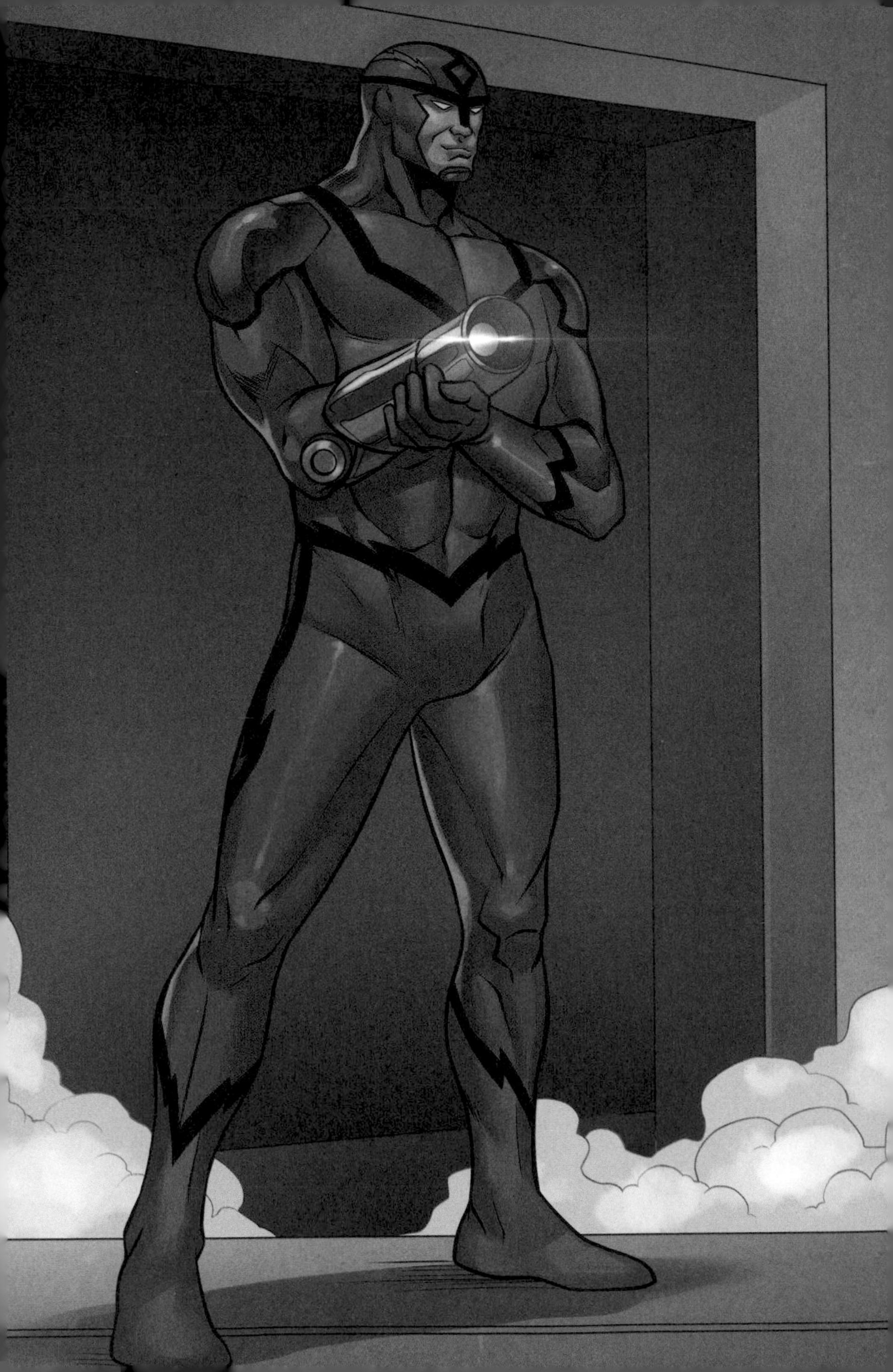

"**Klaw**," growled Black Panther.

"**TOOK YOU LONG ENOUGH,**" Klaw scoffed. "**I'VE BEEN WAITING FOR THIS MOMENT.**" The decoy handed him the two metal bracelets it had stolen. Klaw calmly snapped them into his wrist gauntlet. His eyes lit up as a jolt of power rippled through his body. "**YOU'RE DISMISSED,**" Klaw said, patting the decoy on the head. The android took a step back and deactivated itself.

The Avengers burst into the cellblock, War Machine fired off a barrage of missiles. Klaw bombarded the missiles with sound, causing them to explode in midair.

"**THE DEVICES THAT DECOY STOLE FOR ME NOT ONLY PROTECT ME FROM THE EFFECTS OF VIBRANIUM, THEY ALSO ENHANCE MY SONIC ABILITIES. I'M MORE POWERFUL THAN EVER,**"

HE RELEASED A CRIPPLING SOUND BLAST
FROM HIS WRIST GAUNTLET.
THE AVENGERS FELL TO THEIR
KNEES IN AGONIZING PAIN.

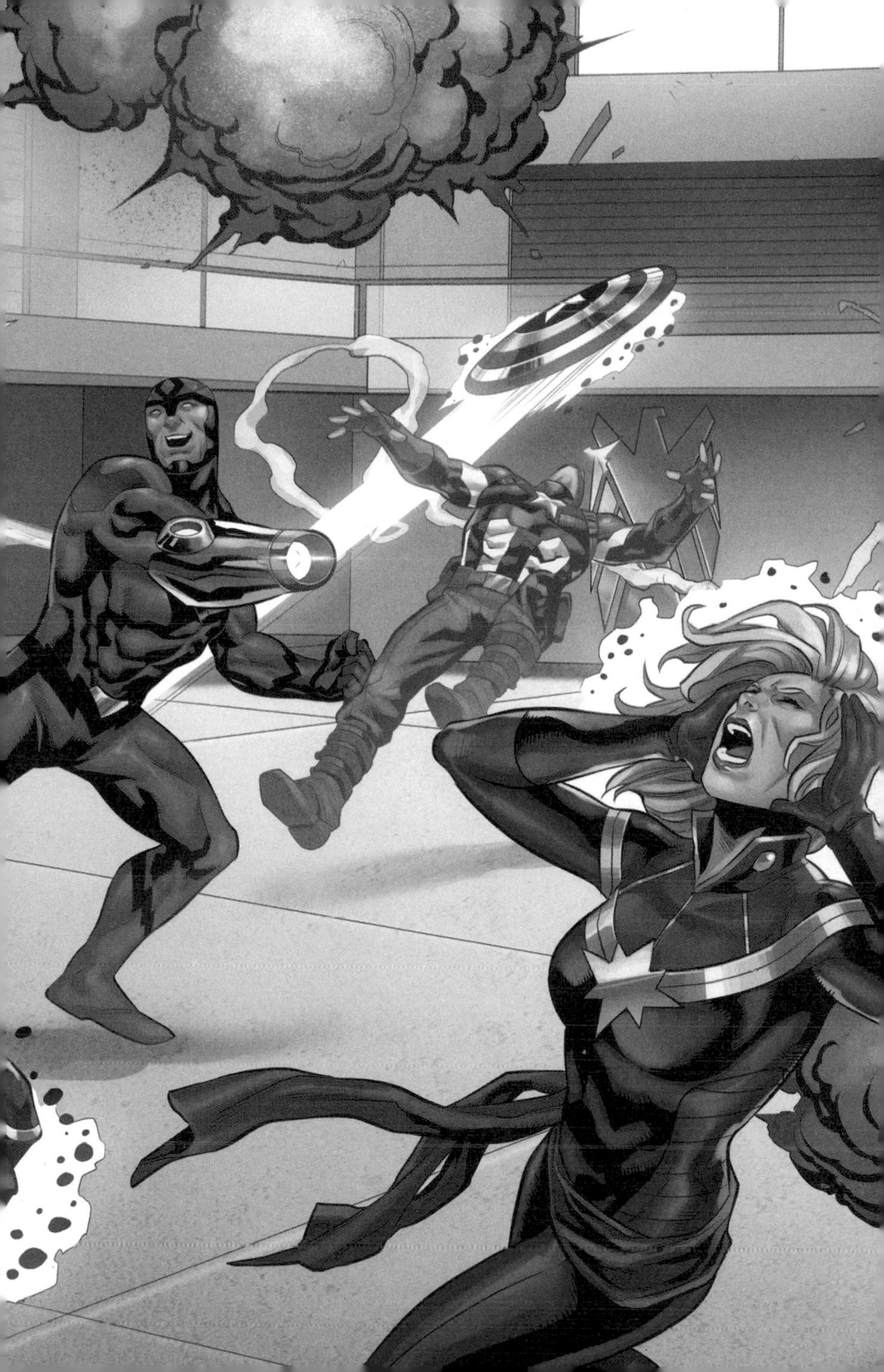

Klaw located the cellblock's communication console and opened an outside channel. "ANSWER ME THIS, BLACK PANTHER. IF YOU'RE HERE AVENGING THINGS, WHO'S WATCHING OVER YOUR KINGDOM? IT'S SUCH A BEAUTIFUL PLACE. I BET THE PEOPLE ARE ANGRY AT THEIR KING FOR LEAVING THEM SO UNPROTECTED."

Black Panther finally realized the scope of Klaw's plan. The revelation took his breath away. "No," gasped Black Panther. "Don't!"

"GOOD-BYE," said Klaw. "I LOOK FORWARD TO HEARING YOU BEG FOR YOUR LIFE." He turned himself into pure sound waves and dissolved into the console. His destination: Wakanda.

"We have to get to Wakanda," the Panther exclaimed. "Now."

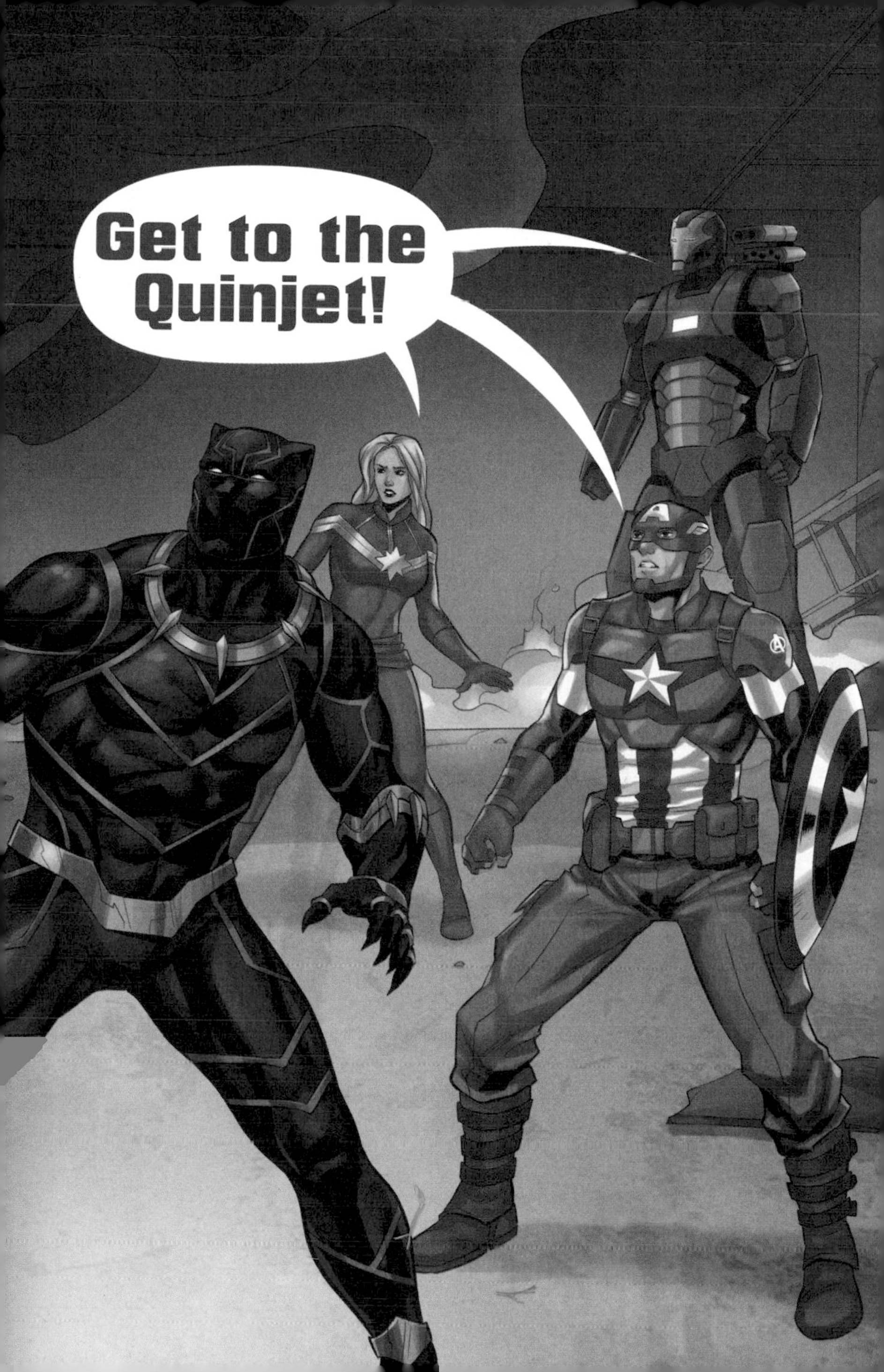
Get to the Quinjet!

they practiced this in a mirror ➜

CHAPTER 7

"Shuri!" the Dora Milaje warrior shouted. **"They are coming!"**

The White Gorilla Cult marched toward the Great Mound with renewed purpose. They were no longer looking to bring only chaos. This time, they were thirsty for blood.

Shuri stood among a handful of Dora Milaje warriors and addressed them with vigor. **"Sisters, I'm here before you today not as a princess but as a warrior! The Great Mound will not fall today. Wakanda will rise!"**

Cheers erupted from the hills as the White Gorilla Cult descended on the Great Mound. Shuri was flanked by two Dora Milaje, Ayo and Aneka. Nakia and Okoye, an additional pair of fighters, stood ready for Shuri's direction.

"Be careful, warriors. Repel these invaders at all costs," Shuri commanded. **"Okoye, stay on the ground. Nakia, watch the skies!"**

As the cultists charged, the Dora Milaje met them with great strength. Nakia vaulted

through the air toward a White Gorilla Cultist. She swiftly scooped him up and tossed him into a deep hole nearby.

TICK, TICK, TICK. BOOM!

An explosion rocked the Mound. Shuri spotted the culprit attempting an escape. She quickly reached for her bolo, a long cord with weighted spheres on either end. Shuri tossed it at the fleeing cultist. The bolo wrapped itself around his feet, causing him to fall to the ground in a tangle.

The Dora Milaje battled back as many cultists as they could, but time was running out. They needed reinforcements.

BEEP! BEEP! BEEP!

Shuri received a distress call from Black Panther. Before she could respond, a cultist lunged in her direction. Shuri dodged the attack and braced herself for the next one. "T'Challa, I'm surrounded by White Gorilla Cultists at the moment," she said, activating her ear receiver. **"What's going on?"** Another cultist surprised Shuri from behind. He ripped the receiver out of her ear and tossed it to the ground. Shuri gave her attacker a swift strike to the chest. He landed on the ground unconscious.

"Klaw is coming!" Black Panther shouted. "You must be careful."

Shuri was unable to hear her brother's warning. Before she could grab the receiver, a monstrous foot stomped it to pieces as a beastly shadow fell upon the area. Shuri looked up to find the fearsome M'BAKU, leader of the White Gorilla Cult. He snarled at Shuri and panted like an animal. His ferocity was legend.

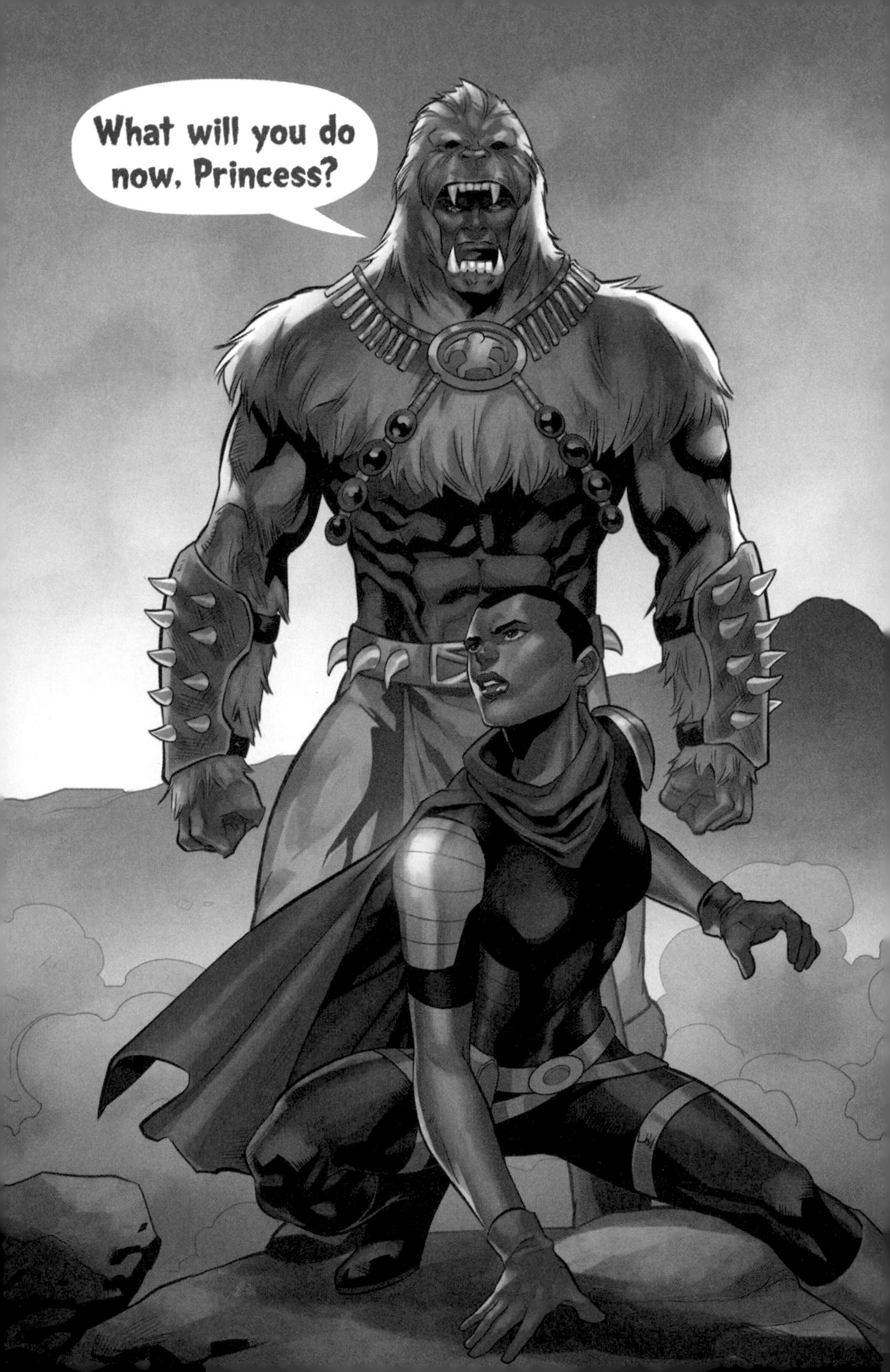
What will you do now, Princess?

"**This!**" Shuri said, kicking M'Baku in the knee. He remained unmoved.

"**Ha ha ha! You have spirit, little girl,**" M'Baku cackled. "**I will destroy it.**" He picked Shuri up by the shoulders and moved his face close to hers. M'Baku's foul breath made her wince in disgust.

ROAR!

"**You don't scare me.**" Shuri smiled. She head-butted M'Baku with great force. The blow caused him to drop her. She landed on the ground with grace.

"**M'Baku,**" a cultist shouted, pointing to the Quinjet high in the sky. Black Panther and **the Avengers** had arrived. The cultists quickly scattered in all directions.

"**Come back here, you weak fools!**" M'Baku roared. "**What are you scared of?!**"

As the Quinjet descended from above, Black Panther catapulted himself out of its cockpit.

"You and your cult are done," Black Panther shouted.

Black Panther vaulted himself toward M'Baku, delivering strike after strike at incredible speed. The barrage of blows left M'Baku unable to catch his breath.

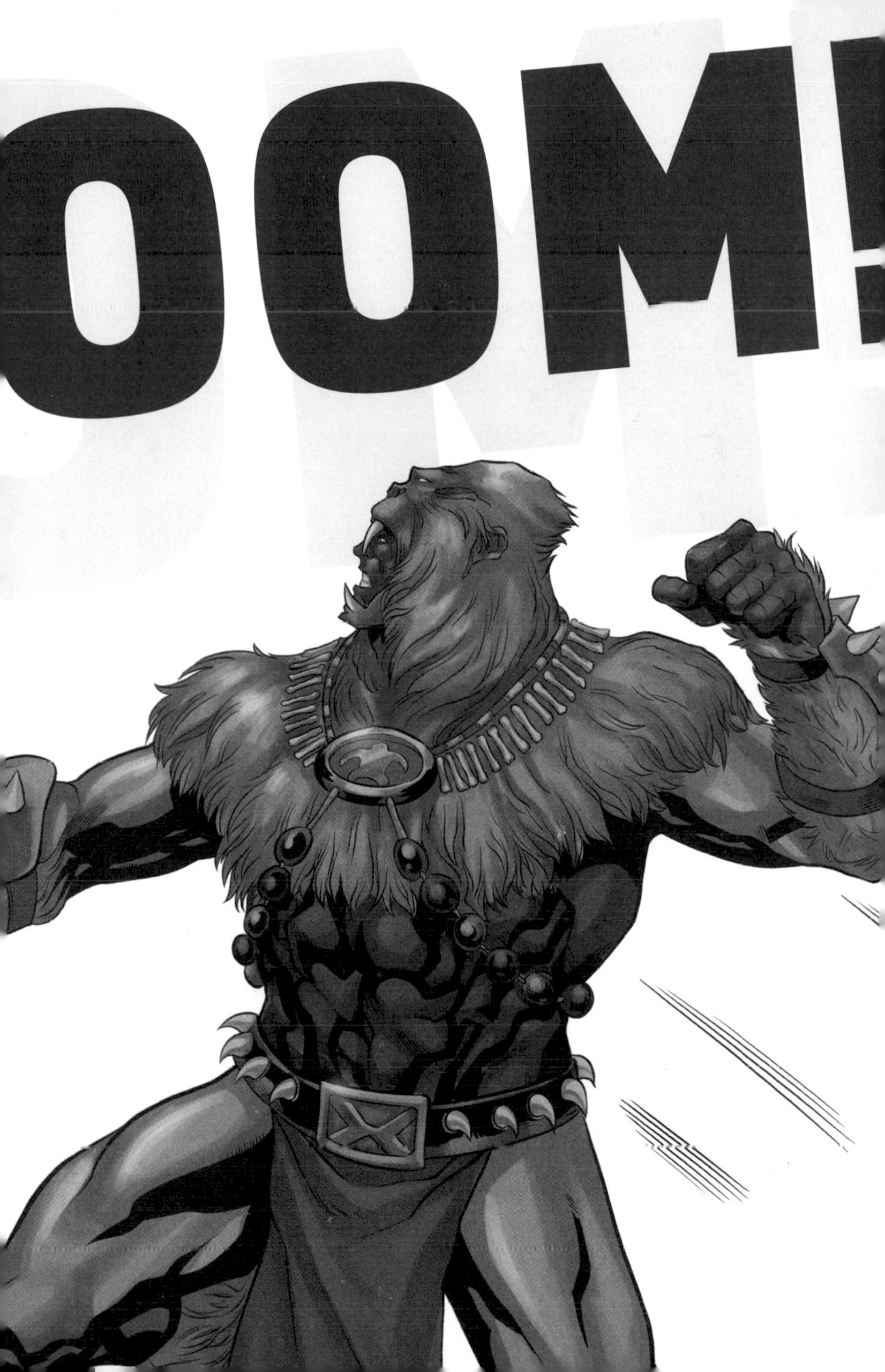
OOM!

The White Gorilla Cultists watched as their leader's enormous frame crashed to the ground in defeat. The battle was over. The Dora Milaje rushed to secure their new prisoners.

"T'Challa!" Shuri exclaimed. She ran to her brother and hugged him hard.

"Klaw is in Wakanda," Black Panther said.

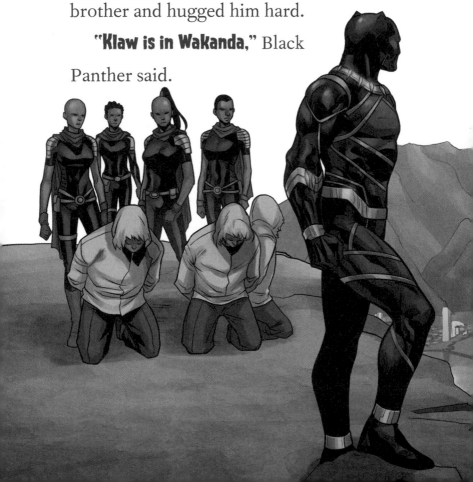

The color left Shuri's face. **"What?"** she muttered.

"There's nothing to fear. Listen closely," Black Panther said. **"I need you to clear the Mound. Get everyone away from here, then join the Avengers. Can you do that?"**

"Yes, but where's Klaw?" Shuri asked. **"What are you going to do?"**

Black Panther looked toward the Golden City. The final game had begun.

CHAPTER 8

FZZZT! SHAZACK!

Deep within the Wakandan royal palace, Klaw made his way through Black Panther's private workshop. He strolled among the many gadgets and inventions, destroying each one as he passed. It was in this workshop that Black Panther created the numerous innovations that helped fuel his country's economy. It was a place that held deep meaning, a place where he felt safe.

During the commotion, Black Panther slipped in through a secret door and hid behind a large

iron column. In his hand was a glowing Vibranium energy dagger.

"YOUR SISTER IS A STRONG FIGHTER. SHE'LL MAKE AN EXCELLENT BLACK PANTHER ONCE YOU'RE GONE. DON'T THINK I COULDN'T HEAR YOU SKULKING AROUND," said Klaw. "SOUND IS MY CURRENCY, FOOL."

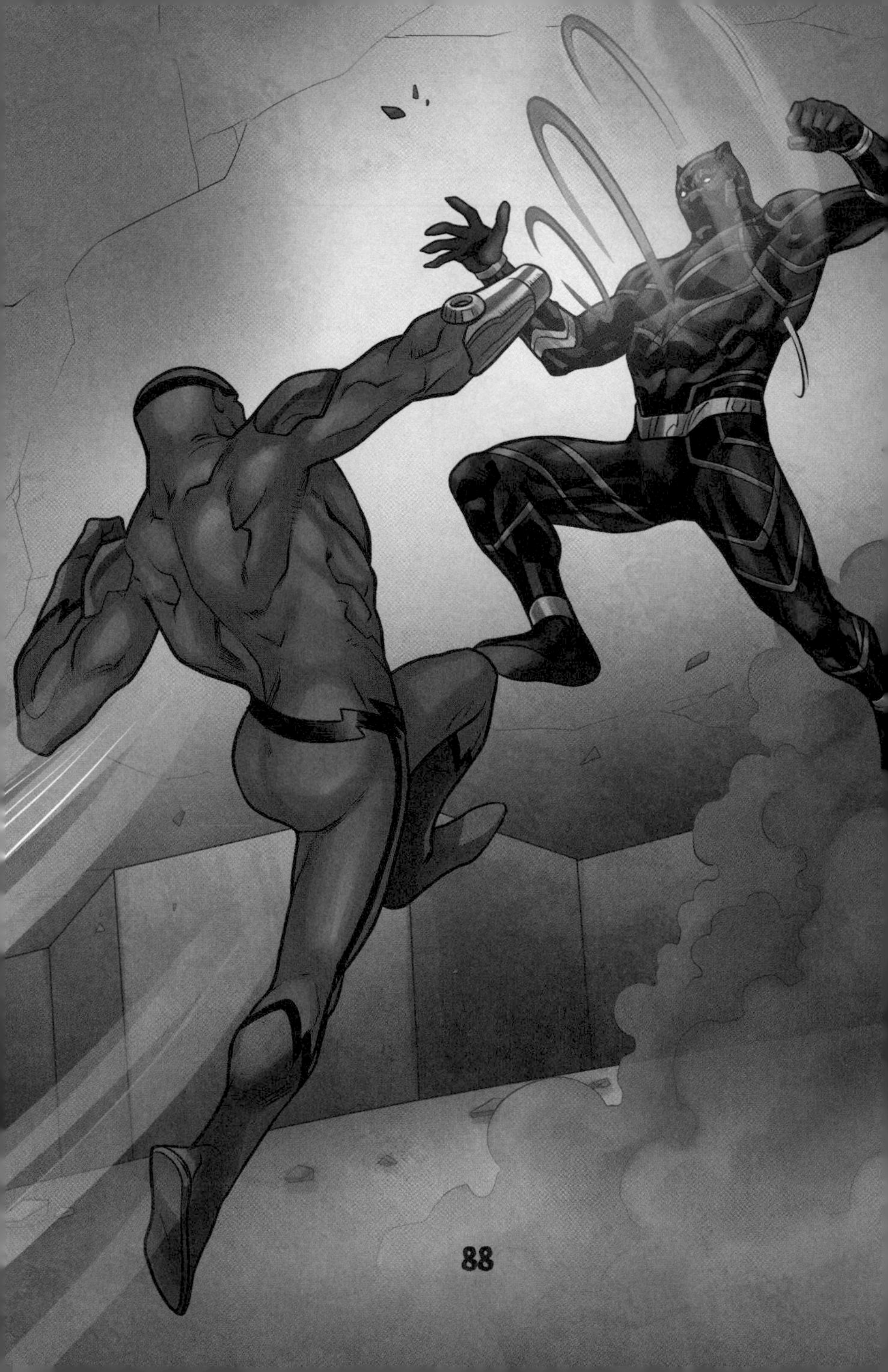

FZZZACK!

Klaw fired off a sonic assault toward Black Panther. The Panther somersaulted across the room, dodging each sound wave with aplomb as Klaw grew irritated. It was a standoff.

"I'm not going anywhere," Black Panther said.

"I'D EXPECT NOTHING LESS, YOU INSUFFERABLE BRAT," said Klaw.

Black Panther threw himself through the air toward Klaw.

BWEEE! BWEEE! BWEEE!

Klaw unleashed a high-pitched frequency that rattled Black Panther's head.

"I'M NOT JUST HERE FOR VIBRANIUM, YOU KNOW. I'M ALSO HERE TO WATCH YOUR PEOPLE TURN AGAINST YOU."

Klaw spoke as Black Panther struggled to stand. "M'BAKU AND HIS WHITE GORILLA CULT ATTACKED THE GREAT MOUND EVERY TIME YOU LEFT WAKANDA BECAUSE I HIRED THEM TO DO SO. I WANTED THE PEO-

PLE TO REMEMBER THAT YOU'D ABANDONED
THEM IN THEIR TIME OF NEED. WAKANDA
WILL FALL."

"**Never!**" Black Panther exclaimed as he
leaped toward Klaw.

"THAT'S ALL YOU'VE GOT?" asked Klaw.

VUUU! VUUU! VUUU!

Klaw adjusted his wrist gauntlet and created a devastating sound wave that shook the royal palace to its foundation. Black Panther had been studying Klaw's movements and demeanor. *He's quick but his body lacks tension. That means he feels comfortable,* he thought.

"YOUR FATHER ONCE TOLD ME VIBRANIUM WASN'T WAKANDA'S GREATEST RESOURCE. HE SAID IT'S THE PEOPLE THAT MAKE THIS NATION STRONG," Klaw said.

"Never speak of my father," Panther said.

"DO YOU MISS HIM?" asked Klaw. "DON'T ANSWER. I KNOW YOU DO. HE WAS A BETTER KING THAN YOU'LL EVER BE."

"You play mind games," said Black Panther.

"Do what you came here to do or leave."

"HOW DARE YOU?!" Klaw spit back. "YOUR FOOLISHNESS TURNED ME INTO THIS. ALL OF THIS IS YOUR FAULT!"

VUZZZAT! VUZZAT!

Klaw coated the room in a blanket of steady pulsing sound. Black Panther had taken many hits during his years as a hero but never anything like this. To move through the pain, Black Panther turned to meditation, another tool his father had taught him.

93

Whenever he found himself in a stressful situation, Black Panther closed his eyes, cleared his mind, and focused his energy inward.

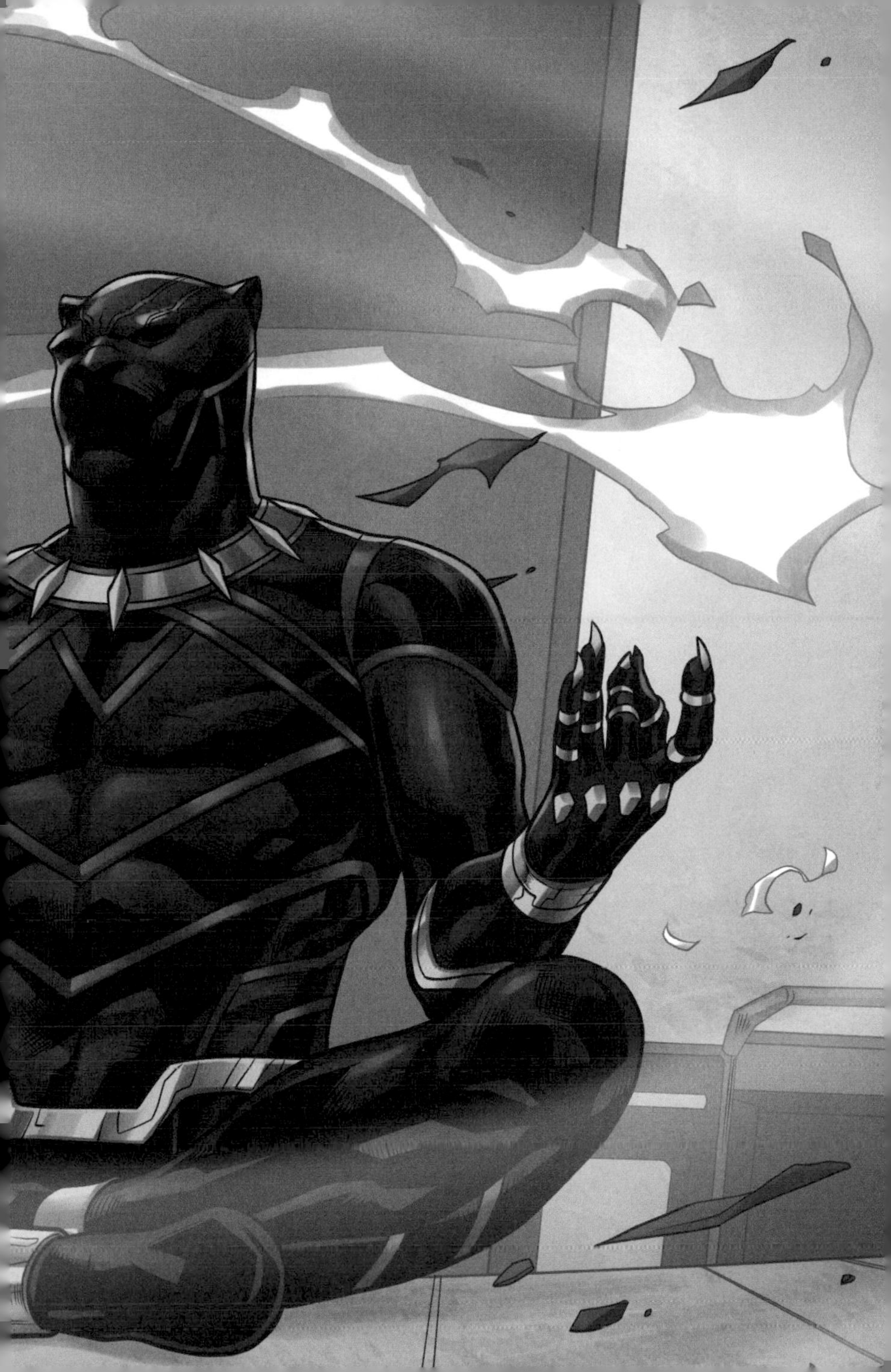

Klaw noticed Black Panther's peaceful silence. "YOU'RE NOT THE THREAT I THOUGHT YOU'D BE. HOW DISAPPOINTING," he said. "WHEN YOU REGAIN YOUR STRENGTH, COME SAY HELLO. YOU KNOW WHERE I'LL BE." Klaw dissolved into the air.

Black Panther opened his eyes and awoke from his meditation.

I know what I must do.

super annoyed →

Black Panther shook his head in disbelief as he sifted through the remnants of his workshop. He couldn't believe his many great achievements had been destroyed in front of his eyes. Now they were broken things that needed fixing. The conflict wasn't over yet. Shuri returned from her task to find her brother among the wreckage.

"We don't have much time," Black Panther said. **"Klaw is expecting me."** His eyes darted through the room, searching for something. He began rummaging through the wreckage.

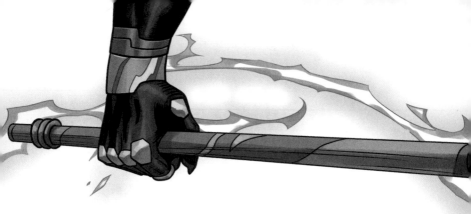

"**Are you all right?**" Shuri asked.

"**I'll survive,**" Black Panther said.

"**What are you going to do?**" Shuri wondered.

"**Keep going,**" Black Panther said. He finally found what he was looking for: a long, magnetic tube. He looked the item over and was pleased. "**Where is Ramonda? Is she safe?**" he asked.

"**Yes. The Great Mound has been cleared but the people are concerned. Where's Klaw? What are you planning to do, brother?**" Shuri said.

Black Panther took off his mask and smiled at his sister.

"**No matter what happens today, Shuri, know**

that I am proud of you. I know our father would be as well," he said.

"You speak as if this is the end, T'Challa," Shuri said.

Just then, the Avengers entered the workshop.

"You should definitely fire your maid," Captain Marvel said.

Captain America was in no mood for jokes. "Stay focused, team. Klaw is at the Great Mound."

"How is that possible? His body would dissolve around Vibranium," Shuri said.

"He acquired technology that protects him.
It's been integrated into his sonic cannon," said
Black Panther.

"I take it you have a plan?" wondered Captain America.

"Of course," replied Black Panther. "But I must confront Klaw alone."

"ARE YOU CRAZY?" War Machine exclaimed.

"I know Klaw better than anyone here," Black Panther explained. "He will see the Avengers coming a mile away. He'll prepare. I must approach him one-on-one."

"He shoots sound. It's not like he's unstoppable," Captain Marvel said. "Let's just blast him and get it over with."

"After Klaw killed my father, I didn't understand what could drive a man to take another's life," Black Panther explained. "I soon realized that Ulysses Klaw is a man that chooses to believe want he wants. I believe this arrogance will lead to his downfall."

"So, what can we do?" asked Captain Marvel.

"You must not be seen. All of you, including Shuri and the Dora Milaje, stand ready with your weapons. When I give the signal, aim for Klaw's sonic wrist gauntlet and open fire."

Captain Marvel noticed the magnetic tube in Black Panther's hand. "What's that for?"

"You'll see," Black Panther replied.

RUMBLE!

Wakanda began to tremble with the power of sound.

RRRUU
UUUMM
MBBBLE

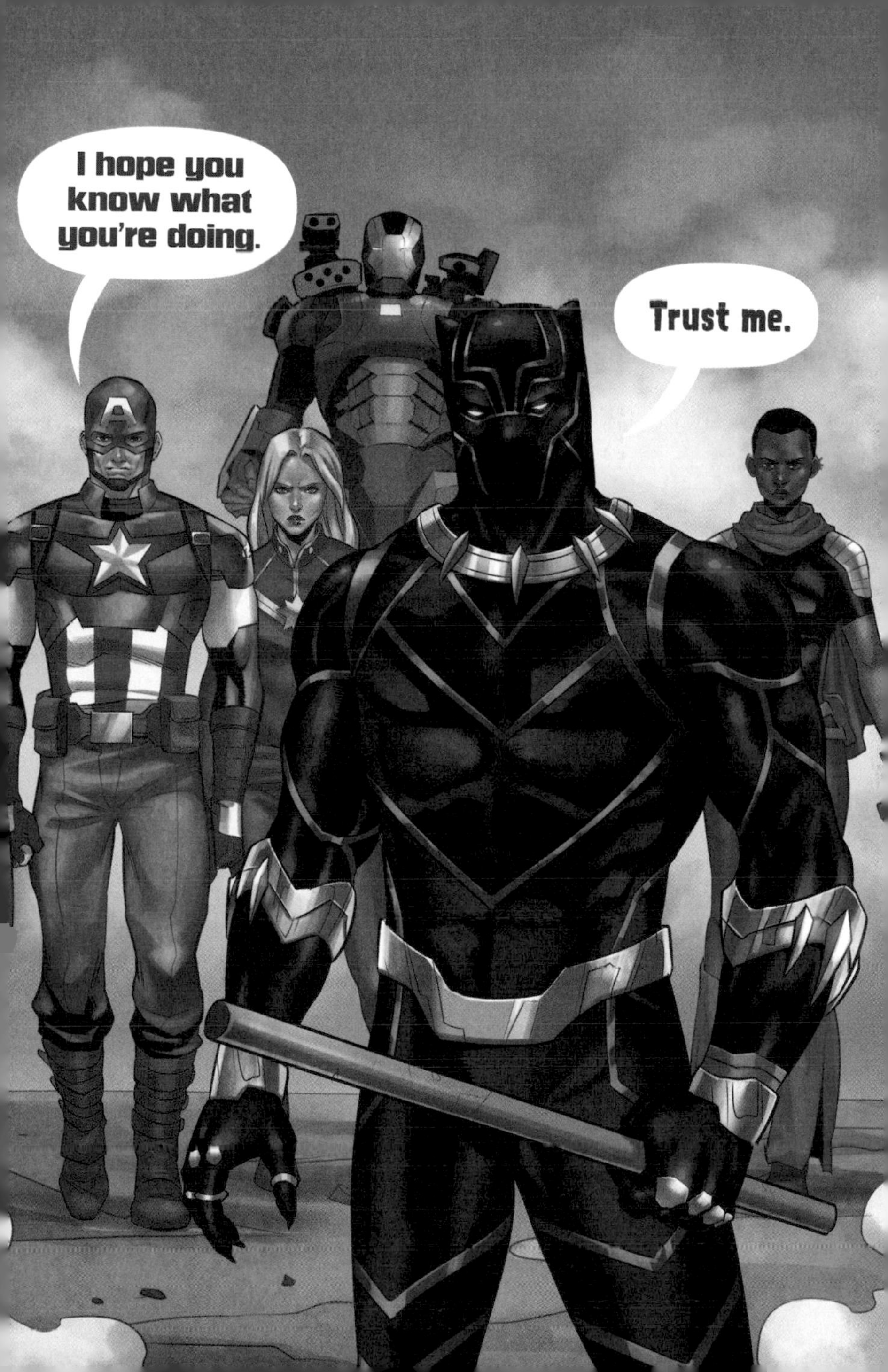
I hope you know what you're doing.
Trust me.

CHAPTER 10

FVZACK!

Klaw stood in the middle of the Great Mound, using his sonic powers to tear it apart. High in the clouds above, War Machine circled with Black Panther in tow.

"Drop me," Black Panther said.

"I KNOW THAT VIBRANIUM SUIT CAN TAKE A BEATING, BUT WE'RE OVER A THOUSAND FEET UP. ARE YOU SURE?" War Machine asked.

Black Panther nodded in the affirmative. War Machine loosened his grip and Black Panther plunged from the sky, landing on the Mound's hillside ledge with a **BOOM!**

Klaw grinned. A mechanical hum filled the air as pure sound energy pulsed through his body.

SHATHOOM!

He blasted the rock underneath Black Panther's feet, causing him to fall from the hillside amid a flurry of rubble.

Black Panther pulled himself from the rock pile and stumbled to his feet. Black Panther's master plan was taking shape.

SHAZACK!

Klaw attacked again. **"I WILL TAKE YOUR GREATEST RESOURCE AND I WILL DESTROY YOU WITH IT!"** he barked. **"THEN I WILL COME FOR**

YOUR PEOPLE." He laid his hand on the ground and focused his power, using it to create an earthquake. Vibranium churned deep below the earth as a series of tremors vibrated outward toward the whole of Wakanda. The Great Mound shook with violent force as it began to crumble to pieces.

"Klaw!" Black Panther shouted. **"Stop!"**

Klaw paused. A maniacal grin developed on his face. **"SURRENDER. SURRENDER TO ME!!!"**

Black Panther tried to keep himself balanced on the trembling Earth. Klaw's tremors were making the ground crumble beneath him. Then, Black Panther slowly raised his hands in the air. But it wasn't a surrender—it was the signal. In the blink of an eye, Shuri, the Dora Milaje, and the Avengers rose from the edges of the Great Mound. Black Panther smirked.

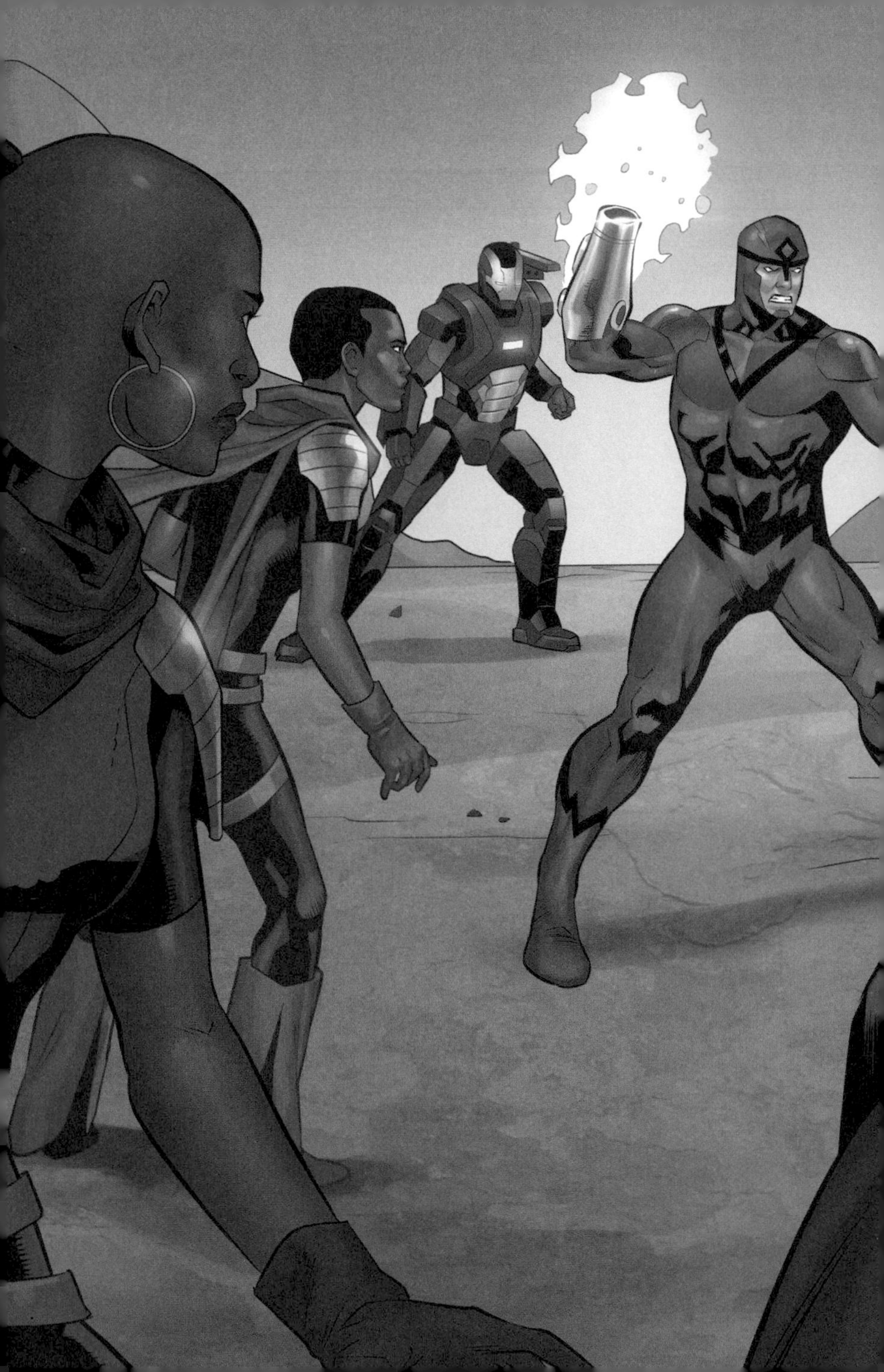

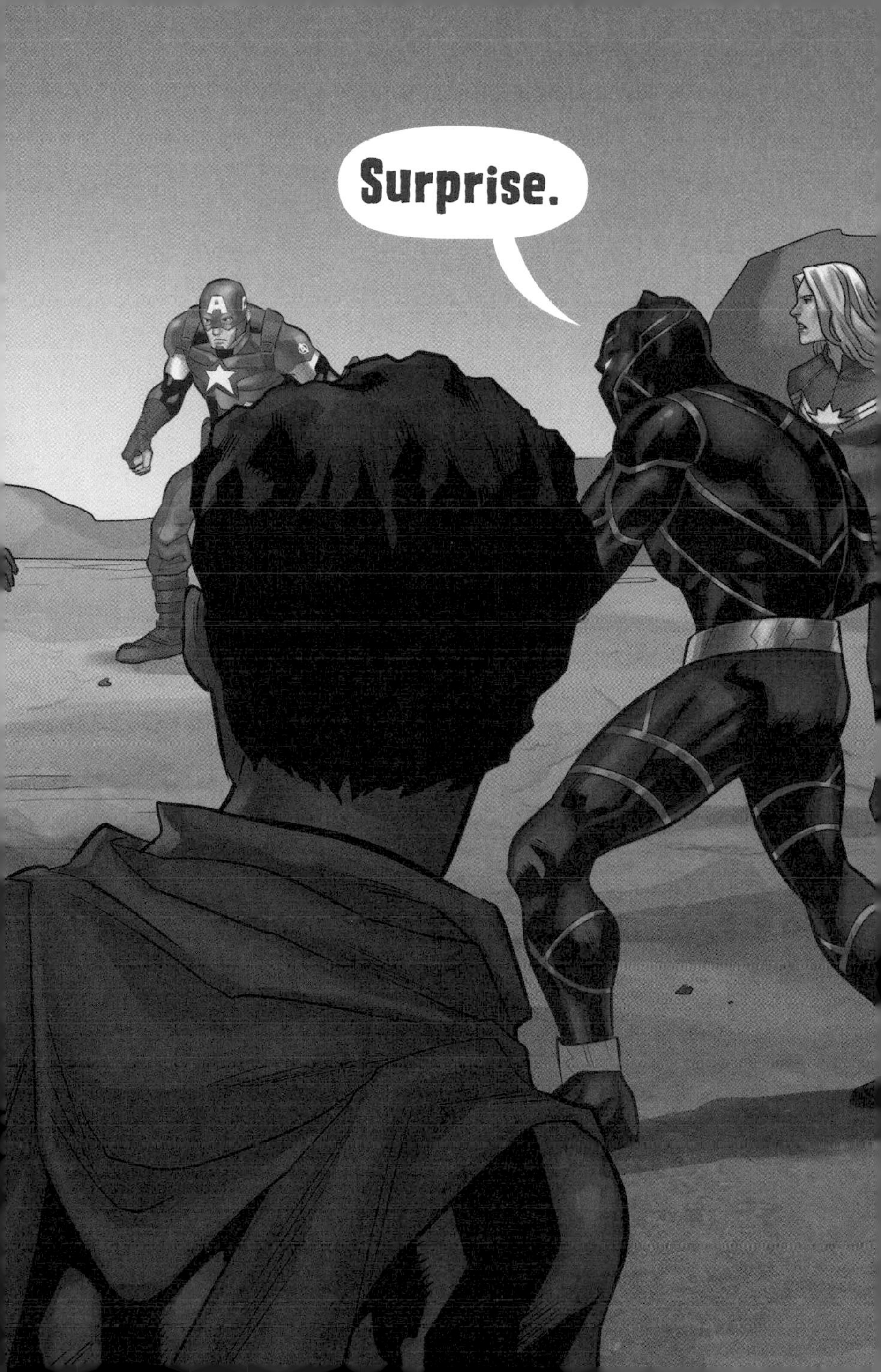
Surprise.

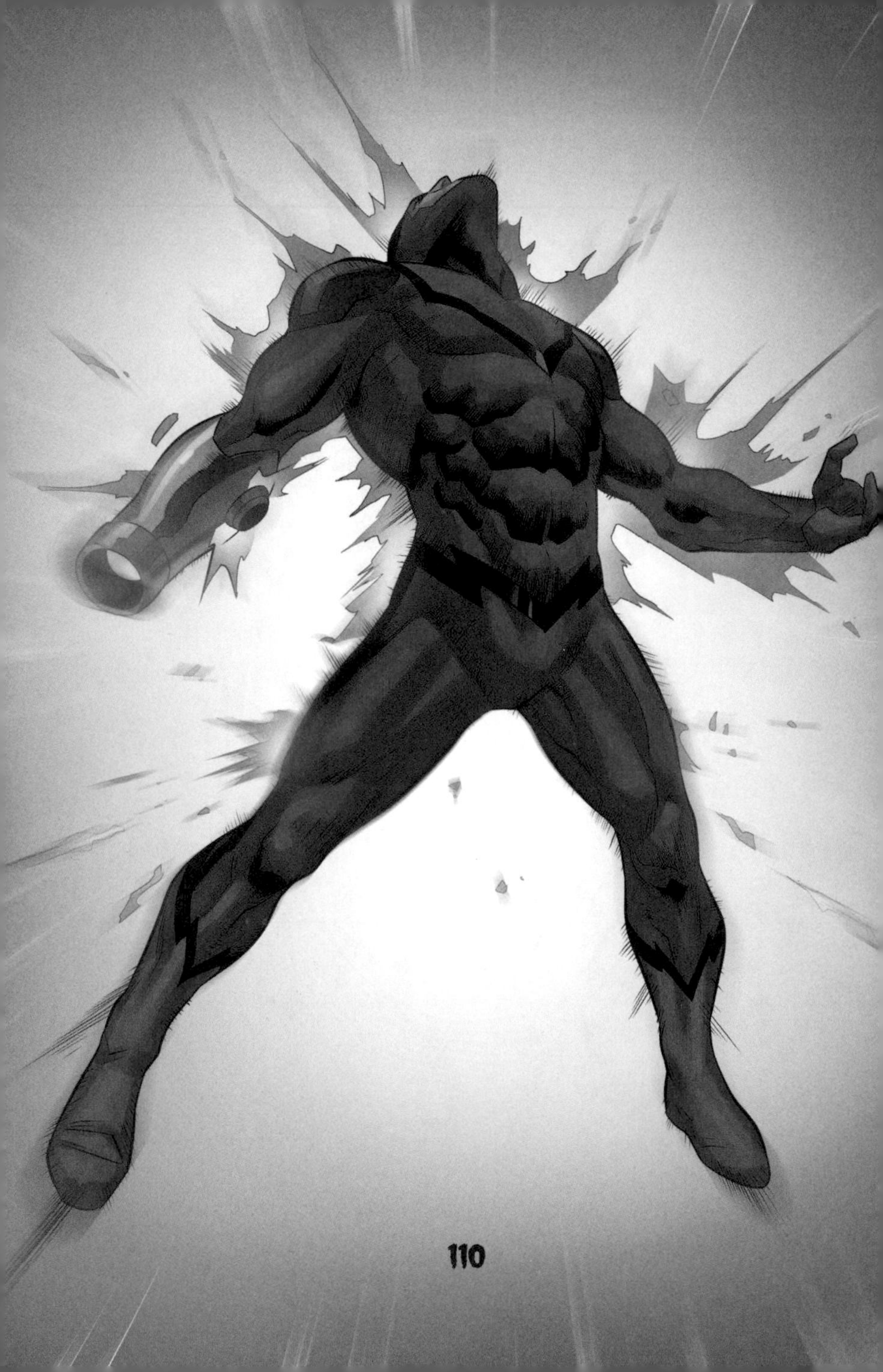

All at once, the heroes fired their weapons. Klaw was caught unaware. His wrist gauntlet shattered as his scream echoed throughout the kingdom. With his safeguards destroyed, the Vibranium within the Great Mound overwhelmed Klaw's physical form. Black Panther grabbed the magnetic tube, capturing Klaw's sound.

"This tube keeps Klaw in a state of constant unrest, leaving him unable to reassemble into his physical form," Black Panther explained.

Captain America was in a state of disbelief. **"Klaw hit you with everything he had."**

"That's what I was counting on," Black Panther said.

"Why endure all of that?" Captain Marvel asked.

"Enduring is what I do," Black Panther said. He looked out among the hills and noticed the citizens of Wakanda had assembled.

"They must have heard the commotion," Shuri said.

The people looked upon their king's bravery. They saw his commitment to defending Wakanda, and their spirit was renewed. Then a curious thing happened. The crowd parted to reveal T'Challa's mother, Ramonda. She walked over and stood

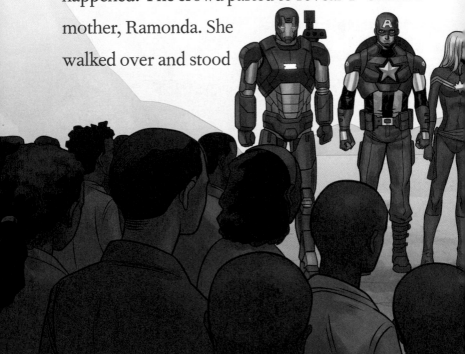

at his side. **"Like your father would say, it's the people of Wakanda that make this nation strong."**

Black Panther prepared to speak to his people, but before he could begin, Ramonda leaned into his ear with a reminder. **"Take your mask off, son."**

"Thank you, Mother," T'Challa said, removing his mask. He took a breath and began. **"Wakandans, forces within our nation conspired**

to instill fear in our people through violence and terror. These forces have been dealt with. We are safe once again. Wakanda is grateful for the protection offered by the Dora Milaje. That's why my sister, Shuri, will take an active role in their development."

Shuri's eyes widened. She hadn't expected such an announcement. Her brother continued.

"The Avengers are my teammates. They defended our nation as if it were their own. I'm thankful to be among their ranks. Furthermore, Wakanda is not a world unto itself. We must bridge the gap between us and other cultures. In the coming weeks, I will invite representatives from the other nations of the world to see Wakanda for themselves. We are not a country of secrets. Lastly, I wish to mention my father, T'Chaka. He

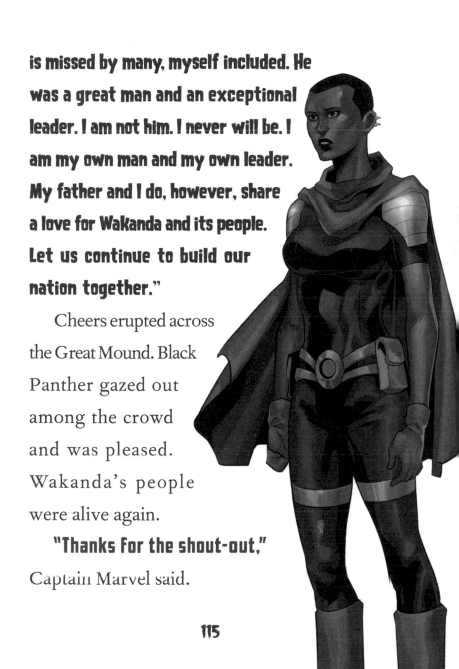

is missed by many, myself included. He was a great man and an exceptional leader. I am not him. I never will be. I am my own man and my own leader. My father and I do, however, share a love for Wakanda and its people. Let us continue to build our nation together."

Cheers erupted across the Great Mound. Black Panther gazed out among the crowd and was pleased. Wakanda's people were alive again.

"Thanks for the shout-out," Captain Marvel said.

"Rest assured, T'Challa, Nick Fury and I are going to have a conversation. Whether he likes it or not," Captain America said, smiling. "The Avengers are there to help S.H.I.E.L.D. defend the world, but we don't follow orders blindly. Only by trusting each other will we be able to work together and move forward. Thanks for reminding me of that."

"CAN I MOVE HERE? I PROMISE I'LL BE A GREAT ROOMMATE. ALL I NEED IS A BED AND A WINDOW, I SWEAR," War Machine joked. "AND MAYBE A BATHROOM."

"Thank you, all," Black Panther said. "For everything." The Avengers boarded the Quinjet and ascended into the sky. Ramonda and T'Challa retired to the royal palace for some well-deserved peace and quiet.

"How are you, son?" Ramonda asked.

T'Challa thought for a moment. In the past day he'd wrestled with cultists, tracked down his imposter, and faced his greatest enemy in battle. Even for a Super Hero, he'd experienced quite a lot.

Despite the dangerous situations he'd recently been through, T'Challa felt complete.

BBFs for life

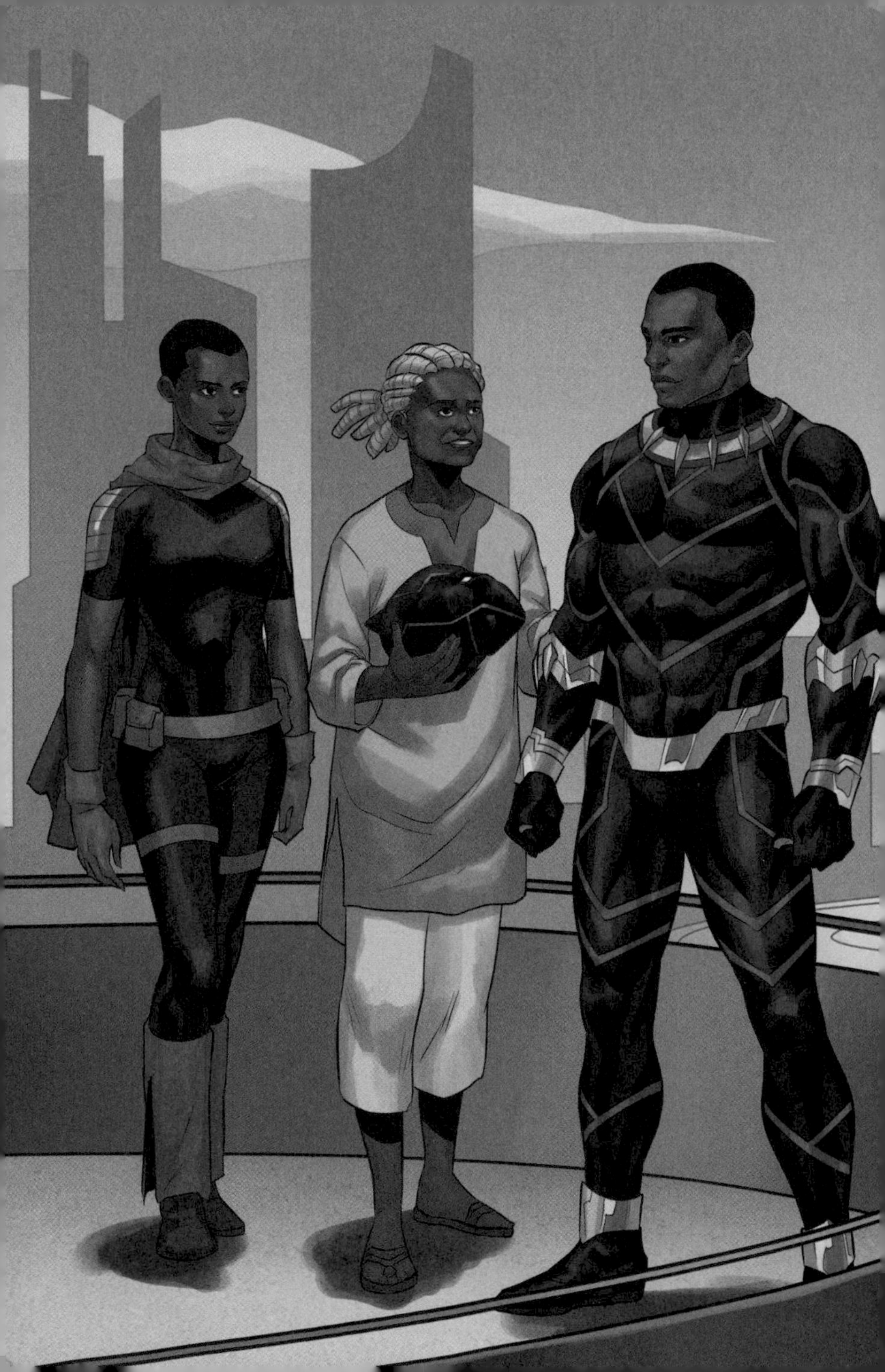

"Hope springs eternal," T'Challa said.

Shuri burst into the room. **"Oh! I didn't mean to interrupt,"** she said.

"Come in, dear," Ramonda said.

"I was thinking of heading out to Warrior Falls for a training session," Shuri said.

T'Challa gave a long sigh and then shot Shuri a devilish look. **"Race you?"**

"Only if I can have a head start," Shuri said, rushing out of the room.

"T'Challa, can you not just rest?" Ramonda asked.

"Not really," T'Challa said, and smiled.

He put his mask on and leaped off the balcony into the brush below. The people of Wakanda could now rest easy because the Black Panther was on the prowl once again.

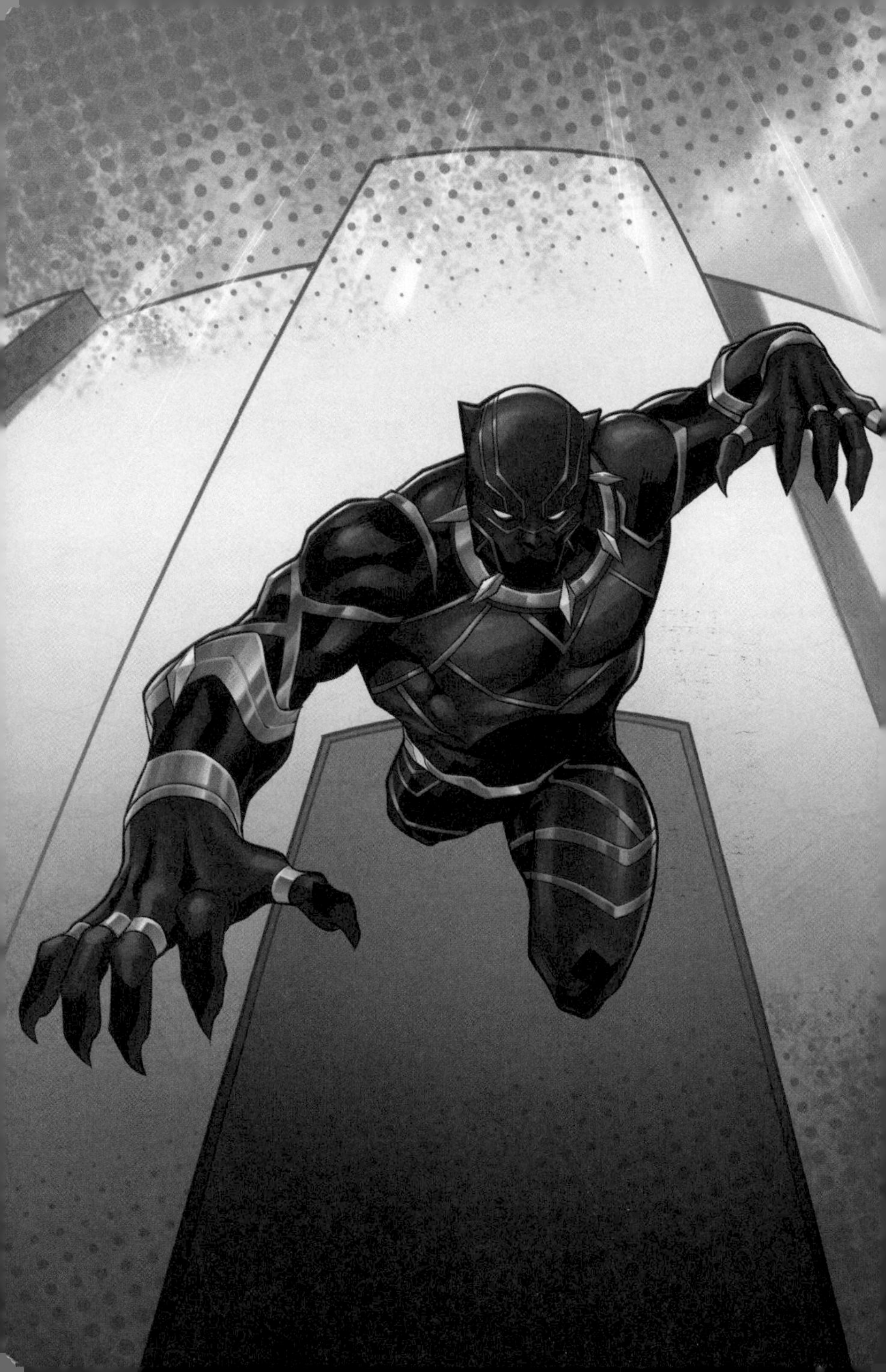